About the author

Will Gatti has always been passionate about stories and storytelling – which didn't help him much at school as he spent much of his time daydreaming. He went off to university and fell in love with an Irish girl and Ireland. After marrying the girl he went to live in France where he did a variety of jobs, including being a docker.

After spending some time working in London doing various things, including playing in a band, working for a publisher and teaching, Will went off to the west coast of Ireland with his young family. It was there that he started his writing career.

Will is now head of English in a school in Surrey, but between marking essays and in the school holidays he finds time to write. *The Geek, the Greek and the Pimpernel* is his seventh novel.

THE Geek,

THE Greek

AND THE

P*impernel

FOR EVA, NONNA AND MUM,
WHO COULD DO THE PIMPERNEL
LAUGH BETTER THAN ANYONE

ORCHARD BOOKS
338 Euston Road, London NW1 3BH
Orchard Books Australia
Level 17/207 Kent St, Sydney, NSW 2000

A Paperback Original
First published in Great Britain in 2007
Copyright © Will Gatti 2007

The right of Will Gatti to be identified as the author of this work has been asserted
by him in accordance with Copyright, Designs and Patents Act, 1988.

A CIP catalogue record for this book is available from the British Library.

ISBN 978 1 84616 367 8

3 5 7 9 10 8 6 4 2

Printed in Great Britain

The paper and board used in this paperback are natural recyclable products
made from wood grown in sustainable forests. The manufacturing processes conform
to the environmental regulations of the country of origin.

Orchard Books is a division of Hachette Children's Books, an Hachette Livre UK company

www.orchardbooks.co.uk

THE Geek, THE Greek AND THE Pimpernel

Will Gatti

ORCHARD BOOKS

Chapter 1

Up the long hill to school.

Head down, collar up.

First day of term.

Don't say boo to a goose, not that there are any geese in my school. Monsters, maniacs and muggers is what we have, not a single goose.

The pavement is wet and slippy and the wind is cold. Stuff hands into pockets and walk a little quicker.

'Oi! It's the Trokka!'

The slap of fat feet and more shouting. What did I say: monsters, maniacs and muggers and here they are: the JACO BIN gang, so called because they love to stuff their victim's head down into a dustbin; and it's Jaco himself out nice and early, seeing what he can pinch from new pupils or harmless citizens like me. A deep breath.

'Trokka!'

That's what they call me. My real name's Michael Patroclus but that's worse than a mouthful of pebbles to geniuses like Jaco, that's why they call me Trokka.

I don't stop, but I don't start running either.

'Got some chocca, Trokka?'

Jaco laughs. He thinks he's a comic genius, he does. He has two of his mates jostled up beside him, grinning the way I imagine wolves grin when they are moving in for the kill. Jaco grins too but his little piggy eyes look right through me, checking to see whether I'm scared or not. But I keep the mask on, the Trokka mask. The outside me. Don't let them know what's going on inside. 'Well?' he says, sticking out his hand.

'I haven't got any.'

'The Trokka's got no chocca,' he says in a pretend surprised voice, and then suddenly leans towards me and pokes my top pocket. 'Wotsis? Wotsis? Wotsis?'

It's a bar of chocolate of course. I always keep one there so the muggers have got something to pinch.

Better to lose a bar of chocolate than get your head stuck in a dustbin. My family is Greek, you see, and Greeks are famous for being smart, making deals and cunning plans and fooling our enemies. This is what my father says, but then my father likes to make a lot of noise and sing and smash plates when he is happy, so I don't always listen to him, but fooling enemies, this I do all the time.

'Well, well.' Jaco's left hand grabs my collar and pulls me a little closer, his right hand scrubbles into my pocket and removes the bar. 'Don't mind if we do, Trokka.'

'Don't mind at all,' chorus the cronies. The one on the left is called Stef. He's got crooked teeth and he's so stupid that I think even Jaco gets fed up with him. But a boy like Jaco has to have a gang; numbers are more important than brains to someone like him.

'Thought you'd keep it from us, did you, Trokka?' says Stef.

I ignore him. Jaco is studying me while taking a chomp out of the bar. Jaco is not easily fooled. I give a shrug. 'Mum must have slipped it in my pocket as a treat.'

'Oh yeah? Without telling you?'

'Without telling me.' My voice is flat as a rail track but my heart is beating like a war drum. I want to shout louder than my father; I want to smash plates on Jaco's head but instead I take a breath and look him in the face.

Jaco nods. He knows the score. If you say you've got something and give it over right away, they think you must be hiding something else, something better. And that is not good news. They won't leave you alone till they've been right through everything: pockets turned inside out; bag tipped up; books in the gutter; and your head in a dustbin. So I always keep a bar for the muggers to find; it keeps them happy, mostly.

'Thanks, Trokka.' Jaco gives one square to each of his pals and then saunters off down the hill, Stef and his mate sticking so close they look like they've been super-glued together. That's an idea, super-glue might come in handy one day. The day of my revenge...

My school is just up ahead. At the very top of the hill: tall, sooty-black walls, long, thin windows so smeared with dirt that you'd need X-ray vision to see in or out, and steep roofs peppered with chimney pots teetering up into the sky. Not that you ever see a good fireplace blazing inside. When the sun shines, the school casts a long shadow down over the town. School? It doesn't look like any school you've ever seen. It should be called Hell Hall, or Dracula's Retreat. I'm not kidding. That's the sort of place it is. **Staleways Middle School, for ages seven to thirteen**. The one and only school in Peasely.

Head down. Collar up. Hands deep in my pockets.

Revenge? I dream of it sometimes. Me a hero like Odysseus or the giant Ajax. And then I would Bin them all!

Dream on. You know that story with all those heroes in it, and the Wooden Horse and that? Well, there was a Patroclus there too and he was no hero, ended up dead, skewered like a kebab. No, revenge is about as likely as Jaco and his Bin gang helping old ladies cross the road.

The only thing to do, if you're halfway smart, is to follow the rules. My rules.

These are the rules:

1. Look out for number one. That's me, and my family, and don't mind about anyone else.

2. Keep away from Jaco and the Bins; they like to play 'shove small people in the gutter', and I am small.

3. Keep away from new pupils; they get picked on.

4. Keep away from anyone else trudging up the hill on their own because if they're on their own they're smart like me and won't want company, and if they're not smart then they're sad and are going to latch onto you, hoping you'll be a friendly face.

5. Keep your head down all the time and avoid being noticed. There are no friendly faces in Staleways so don't be a saddo and think there might be. I'm now so good at not being noticed that I'm almost invisible. I know where to sit at lunch, where to hide at break and where to stand in a queue — never at the front but never at the back either. I am Mike Patroclus, Mr Invisible, except when Jaco spots me but that's only on the way to and from school. Once I'm inside I disappear. I'm one of the mice, not one of the blind ones that get their tails chopped off with a carving knife, but one of the two or three pupils small and grey and cunning enough to keep out of trouble.

6. Never show what you feel.

7. Always keep a choc bar in the top right pocket, but you know about that. And keep a second bar too, well hidden. I've a pocket inside my shirt that Dad sewed for me. I'll eat it in Mr Dorner's lesson after break; he's so unhappy he hardly ever notices anything.

8. And last and most importantly, don't let anyone, especially Mr Pent, the headmaster, know that you can think. Clever children who like to do their work get punished all the time. So, unless you want to spend your Saturday mornings in the Swotshop – we're all swots, that's what they call us – doing Mr Pent's special detention, you stay as invisible as you can. The Swotshop's downstairs, below ground level, like a dungeon. And no one talks about it! No one says the word, 'Swotshop', no one. Bad luck. Say it and, as sure as hell is hot, you'll end up there the very next Saturday morning.

So this is it, first day of my last year. Twelve weeks to get through till Christmas. Not so bad if you stick to the rules, my rules.

That's what I told myself as I slogged up the long hill.

Of course I was wrong. If I knew the future I would be Mr Double Smart, but you can't know the future till you've been there. As it happens my future was a geeky looking girl, and this other new pupil in my year.

Let me tell you about him.

Let me tell you about him and the whole crazy mystery that turned Staleways, prison school from hell, upside down.

Chapter 2

First things first.

In we go through the school's huge black double doors and there's Mr Robestone, the deputy. He's got a weasel face, a nose like a spike and teeth that don't fit in his mouth. A monster? Of course he is, and he has his own private police. There are two of them beside him, red scarves round their necks, their arms folded. Other schools have prefects. We have Robestone's militia. They do the ear pulling, the shouting in your face, the upending, and the dustbin dumping.

Have you guessed who they are? Jaco's Bins of course. They're easy to spot because they've all got a red neck scarf, except some of them wear the scarves like a bandana, and others like Jaco wear them in a tight band round their right arm. They can do what they like, the Bins, and none of the other teachers will say boo to them. All they have to do is obey Mr Robestone.

'Swots!'

That's us, everyone that's not a Bin.

'Oi you, shovel face, in a line!'

'First formers up the front.'

'Do that again, sunshine, and you're binned.'

I can feel Robestone's eyes scanning us all as we come in through the doors but I keep my head down and let myself get jostled along into the big hall for assembly. We're shovelled into rows, little ones at the front, me and my year at the back, the Bins lounging along the walls.

It's a creepy place, the hall. There are skinny windows at the far end that let in dusty shafts of light. One of them has coloured glass and the light that comes in from that one looks like it's been stained with blood.

Jaco comes in and stands at the end of my row. He gives a grin. 'Thanks for the chocca. Here.' He beckons me to come out of the line and stand beside him.

Not a good idea. I stick where I am, staring at the ground, pretending I didn't hear.

'Oi!' The smile's gone and he's pointing. 'Out

15

here, Trokka, now!'

The pupil standing next to me mutters, 'Better do what you're told, Patroclus.' And who's she! Some geeky new girl I've never seen before. So much for me being Mr Hidden.

The girl edges back a half pace to let me by. She's the ultimate Geek Girl, all right: all neat and buttoned up, but with wiry hair fuzzed out like a weird halo and big serious eyes.

A boy the other side of her glances quickly my way, his eyebrows lifting a fraction. Another new swot. Don't even know why I notice him. Mr Ordinary, like me, maybe. 'Maybe he'll offer you a job,' says the girl. What's that supposed to mean? But before I can tell her it's best to mind your own business in this place, Jaco reaches in, grabs my arm and yanks me out.

'Chips on Fridays, Trokka,' he says.

I switch to survival mode and look blank. I don't know what he's on about.

'Doesn't your dad still have a café?' I nod. 'And don't cafés do chips?' I shrug. He ignores this. 'And don't boys like me still need chips on account of all the hard work we do helping to run the school smooth?' His mate Stef gives a snort of laughter. 'Well, Trokka, what do you say? A little business arrangement. We go to your dad's café and he gives us free chips. Simple. What do you say?'

My mind spins. What will my dad say? He hates all these bullies. But on the other hand if it means they'll leave me alone... This could be a good thing. A smart deal. He gives me a shake. 'Wake up, Trokka!'

'Don't know,' I mumble. My father says: *you want to make a smart deal, not pay too much? Then what you do is you sound like you don't care. OK?*

'Then ask your dad, Trokka.' He half turns away like that's it. Then he turns back again and gives my lapel a yank so I'm up on my tiptoes, 'No, don't ask him; tell him!'

Then he gives me a savage push so I go staggering backwards down the line and I'm about to fall flat on my back when Geek Girl grabs my arm and pulls me up and into my place.

'Thanks.'

'Off my foot!' she hisses.

'Sorry.' She's really funny looking: eyes huge as cannonballs behind those glasses.

'They didn't offer you a job then?'

Maybe I pull a face because she mouths, 'It was a joke.'

Who tells jokes in Staleways! 'How'd you know

my name?'

'I was just behind you when they nicked your chocolate.'

I look at her out of the corner of my eye. She's staring straight ahead, frowning at the coloured window.

'But they didn't call me by my proper name. They didn't call me Patroclus.'

'My mum likes Greek food.'

'Oh.' I love Greek food. I love to cook too; all my family does. My father is the one, though. He says things like, 'This food, Michael,' holding up a big fat tomato from Greece, 'is food of the gods.' He's always saying stuff like that. 'People who like our food have Greek souls.' It's nonsense but I sort of believe it.

Geek Girl gives a smile and then says: 'I think it sucks though.'

Before I can put her right there's a shout from the stage: 'Silence in the hall!'

All Jaco's thugs straighten up and glare at us lot. Robestone and the rest of Staleways' staff march down the middle and then range themselves in a semicircle up on the stage. Robestone and the two Bins who'd been standing beside him move back to leave the centre free for the headmaster.

The hall's so quiet you could hear a mouse squeak. Then in comes Mr Pent, headmaster, Sir Stephen Pent because he got knighted last year, don't ask me why. Now he's Sir Pent, that's him all right, a slithery snake. And not one of your dull snakes that looks like mud but a spangling, gaudy snake. He likes to look flash, with gold rings and chains and velvet suits, and white shoes with thick crêpe soles so he can sneak round the school spying into the classrooms.

'School,' he says into the microphone, his voice all smooth and whispery like he loves us. 'School, I have some exciting news.'

I glance at Geek Girl and see she's stifling a yawn. She'll have to watch herself for the Bins will begin to notice her.

And then at that moment, the doors at the end of the hall bang open and in comes this boy, just like no one you have ever seen. I suppose he's my age but he is big, bigger than Jaco. He's got sticky-out ears and glasses, like Geek Girl, but with square black frames that make him look like King Nerd from Nerdland, and he's got a grin on his face, like he thinks everybody must love him. He doesn't seem to realise that he has just taken a first and very dangerous step into Mr Pent's jungle. 'Oh,' he says, loud enough for us to hear, 'very sorry. Bit late.' Sir Pent stiffens and straightens up like one of those cobras when it gets ready to bite. 'I had to walk, you see. Dad wouldn't drive me. Is this where I'm meant to be?'

Dad wouldn't drive me! Where does he think he is? No one gets driven to school by their mummy or their daddy, not unless they want to be squelched in mud, bin-dipped and multi-mugged.

He doesn't seem bothered, though. Too dim perhaps to realise the trouble he's stacking up for himself. Some of the younger swots begin to snigger and Sir Pent's important announcement is just about blown away. I see a Bin with a red bandana pushing into the row where the sniggering's coming from and hear a sharp smack. That little corner of the hall goes quiet.

'What's your name, boy?' Sir Pent no longer sounds like he loves anyone. He could turn your bathwater to ice right now.

'Blake,' says the boy, 'Percy Blake.'

'Oh,' says Sir Pent, 'Blake,' his voice suddenly slipping back into its usual oily charm. 'Go and join the end row, if you would.'

Stef and one of his pals, another thug called Maggot, step out from the wall, grinning like apes.

No doubt they reckon Percy Blake will be fun to push around. But somehow, just as they are about to grab him, he steps into the row behind where I'm standing and finds himself a place, leaving Stef goofily pointing his finger at Blake, and Maggot looking like he's been slapped with a wet fish. They look so stupid it's hard not to smile.

'If I can continue,' says Sir Pent, once the hall has gone quiet again, and he starts to tell us about this competition of his.

Chapter 3

Sir Pent's competition sounded fantastic. Well maybe not the competition but the winning prize: a year-long cruise on a luxury liner. Can you imagine? And the liner's a sort of school only with your feet up on a chair and a waiter bringing you a burger and all that luxury stuff. Islands. Blue seas. Dolphins. You name it, he mentioned it.

County radio, local papers, television, Staleways' great competition would be the school event of the year; every pupil in the area could enter. I tell you, Sir Pent mesmerised us. He smiled. He glittered. He waved his hands. We felt so dizzy just looking at him that we almost forgot what kind of a school we were in.

Not me, though. Not for more than half a second. Sir Pent forking out for luxury prizes! No way. Rule number nine: don't believe what they tell you. And this, the more I think about it, has a bad fish smell. Of course I don't say anything. Not that there is much of a chance: class registration follows assembly and then, at last, it's lunch.

We file out, row by row, people murmuring to each other, still excited. Me, I just put my head down. No one would believe me anyway – so let them dream. I'll mind my own business. And I do. Until I get a poke in the back. And another. It's Geek Girl!

'I don't believe it, Patroclus. Do you?' She says it so matter-of-fact, it takes me off guard. That and the way she uses my name like we know each other.

'What's the matter? You're making a funny face.'

'Am I?'

'Oh for heaven's sake.' she makes an impatient gesture. 'Tell me what you think? What's in it for the headmaster?'

She's sharp and I thought she looked the sort who would love competitions. 'Don't know,' I say. The truth is nothing makes sense here. It's always the keen swots who end up in the Swotshop while anyone who does something bad just gets to join Robestone's Bins. I catch sight of one of them looking this way. Maggot. I dig my hands in my pockets and shrink. I don't want trouble, thank you very much. 'Maybe talk later, not now, yeah?' I mutter.

'No talking, you.'

No rule says we can't talk going into lunch, but they can do that, just pick on someone and make them stand in silence.

She ignores me, and even though I have turned around so I'm facing the same way as the queue, she just leans close and keeps going. I sort of knew she would. 'I mean, why such a luxury prize? It'll cost him, the school, a fortune...'

'That's it, you. Button it!'

Maggot, his red scarf so tight round his neck that his eyes are practically popping out of his head, is glaring at Geek Girl. He looks like he wants to strangle her.

But it's like Maggot just doesn't exist. She tugs my arm. Makes me turn round again. 'Look, there's that new boy, Blake. Do you think he needs help?'

He's easy enough to spot. Pupils are swirling around him, hands reaching up to pluck at him, get at his bag most likely. A rich boy's bound to have loads of sweets.

I'm about to tell her that you don't help anyone at Staleways, when Maggot and Stef suddenly grab her, hoick her off her feet and stick her head-first in the bin at the corner of the dining hall.

'I told you, you specky little swot,' rumbles Maggot. Then he and Stef step back out of the way as two members of staff scurry by, not seeing or choosing not to see the legs sticking out of the bin. Kind of skinny they are; they make me think of rhubarb. But rhubarb doesn't wag about and make little muffled squawks.

The queue moves forward, and so do the two Bins. I don't know what makes me stop and help – but I do. A year ago I wouldn't have dreamed of taking such a risk, but she's so skinny and her glasses are so thick, and she only wanted to help the new boy. Before I know it I find myself grabbing her legs and hauling her up.

Her glasses are crooked on her nose and her wiry hair looks as if it's been hit by a hurricane, but apart from that she's in one piece. 'Lucky that the rubbish bins haven't got any rubbish in them yet,' I say.

She doesn't seem upset by the experience at all. She just straightens her glasses and grins. 'Apart from me,' she says.

It's a joke! No one's ever made a joke in Staleways in all the time I've been here – and Geek Girl's made two! Not that it was very funny, but still I am impressed. I grin and then put my finger to my lips. Joke or no joke, I don't fancy getting binned myself.

We follow the queue and find ourselves places at one of the long tables which have the older pupils sitting at it. A few new faces too, not talking to anyone of course, mostly just keeping their heads down and concentrating on their food. I don't pay too much attention to them, though I notice that one of them seems a cool customer, looking around, quietly taking things in; it's the boy who'd been standing next to Geek Girl in assembly. Maybe he's not Mr Ordinary – he's got wax in his hair by the look of it. Not a good idea at all. It doesn't do to be different. But it's mainly the Blake boy, still with that funny dim smile on his face, who catches my eye. He looks like nothing ever bothers him which is just as well because at that moment, Stef and Maggot decide to join our table and Stef deliberately lets his plate full of runny stew trickle down onto Blake's jacket. 'Oh,' he says, 'sorry, my hand must've slipped.'

Maggot goes, 'Hur. Hur.' That's his laugh.

'Perhaps your dad can drive you to the cleaners.' Now I wouldn't count that as a joke at all but it creases up the two Bins – mega brains that they are – and they move down the table a bit and wedge themselves onto the bench.

'Did you see that!' The Geek is almost spitting. Without thinking, I grab her wrist to stop her from jumping up and having a go at them. 'Don't say anything. Not now. Just wait.'

'Wait for what?'

What do I say to that? Wait for a better time, dream-time, my revenge-time. I don't say anything but by then we're all just watching Blake. He's some clown all right. He doesn't seem bothered at all. He just sits and smiles and dabs himself with this super-huge, clean, white handkerchief. 'Dear oh dear,' he says. 'My mum hates me getting food on my clothes.' He really is the prize dimbo. He has the whole table laughing at him but he doesn't seem to mind. I suppose everybody feels safer when there's a new victim in town. Except this was what was so wicked about our first-day-back lunch: Blake didn't turn out to be the victim at all.

There was a fair bit of jostling and noise through lunch, mainly the Bins giving us a bad time whenever a table was called to get its pudding. Then, when it was time for our table to leave, Stef stood up but instead of swinging his leg over the bench and following Maggot out of the room, he sort of half-swivelled, wobbled and then pitched forward so that his face dunked down into a pile of dirty plates. Pure gold. I could hardly believe it, it was so good.

If everyone at the table had found Blake funny before, it was nothing compared to seeing Stef with splats of stew stuck to his nose and cheeks. 'My feet are stuck,' he spluttered. 'Someone's stuck my feet!' When he finally managed to unstick himself and leave the table one of the teachers asked him where his shoes were.

'My trainers are stuck to the floor,' he complained. 'What are you going to do about it, Sir?'

The sir in question wasn't going to do anything about it, but not wanting to have an argument with a thug like Stef, he just ducked his head and scuttled off. Sometimes I think that even the teachers follow my rules.

I peered under the table and there they were. Brilliant! It crossed my mind that maybe someone had put glue under them. But whoever would do something like that? I mean, I know I'd had that thought about super-glue on my way into school; but this was real, not wishful thinking.

I looked up and down the table at all the faces of the boys and girls from my year. Not one of them was any different to me, none of them would say boo – that left the new pupils and of them the only ones I had really paid any attention to were Geek Girl, dim-boy Blake, and that small kid who always seemed to be looking around, not looking down like everyone else. Geek Girl had been beside me throughout the meal so I knew it hadn't been her, but I noticed dim-boy Blake taking off his glasses and ducking under the table to pick something up. Also the other new kid, the small one, left his place for a few minutes. Maybe one of them had done something sneaky.

I looked at Blake again. No, I decided, he was just too dim-looking to do anything like that. And anyway, how on earth would he have known to bring glue with him to school on his very first day? Not possible.

Stef had obviously been trying to work out who the culprit was too. 'If I find out it was one of you lot,' he'd snarled, 'I'll have your guts in a bucket.' Then he'd padded off after his mates. It's a funny thing but a thug doesn't look quite so dangerous when they don't have shoes on and you can see the holes in their socks.

It made me feel good.

In ones and twos the table gradually emptied, till it was just Geek Girl and me sitting there. 'Is school usually this exciting?' she said.

'Not exciting at all,' I said.

'Hm,' she said. Then she got up. 'See you later, Patroclus,' and off she went.

'See you.' Funny – I don't even know her name yet. But she was OK, not really geeky at all. Just different...

I stood up to go too. Afternoon school was about to start and I wanted to make sure that I had my old desk, in my old place, so it was better to get into the classroom before the bell. Then I saw that Blake had left his glasses behind. I picked them up; it wouldn't do any harm to return them to him. But here's the funny thing, the funny second thing; when I had a look at them, just out of nosiness you know, to see how short-sighted the dim boy was, I found that the specs were fake! They were plain glass. Why would anyone want to wear ugly old glasses if they didn't need to? It didn't make sense. But then not much does at this school.

Chapter 4

'Go on!'

That's my dad. He's more excited than anyone by this competition and thinks I should enter. A year-long luxury cruise! His eyes go all watery at the thought of it.

'Of course, Michael, you will win this thing. You will sail to Greece, and see my mother.'

He rubs his hands on his apron and hugs my mum, who pats his cheek.

'It said on the TV, Dad, just for the most gifted. There's no point in me going in for this thing and anyway, you don't really believe it do you? There's bound to be a catch in it somewhere.'

'Catch? What is there to catch? No! It is on television. It is in the newspaper. He cannot cheat with this thing. And he is not so bad as you say; your school does so well. All the time, top marks. Special government money always goes to your school. Believe me, Michael, Mr Pent is a clever man.'

My dad doesn't understand about Sir Pent and what Staleways is really like. It's not that he's stupid and it's not that he doesn't believe me when I tell him things but he believes adults more, and mum is the same; and that has to be the same for all the mums and dads whose children climb up that hill to hell every single day. I wonder what Geek Girl's parents are saying to her. Of course if parents did listen to us, there would be a riot, wouldn't there? Maybe the school would get burned down. And Sir Pent scorched! How good would that be?

But of course they're all going to want to believe Pent, and I'll tell you why: one, there isn't another school in Peasely; and two, it's true, the school does get really good results, just like Dad said. I don't know how it happens: if you try to work, you end up down in the Swotshop in a detention. But the school's a beacon, I read it in the local paper. Beacon? I wish it was a bonfire.

'You will enter,' continues my dad. 'You are a clever boy. You are my son. You will win. Trust me.'

I do – sort of. He and my mother are so happy all the time, it's almost weird. They love to feed people;

they really do. They sing while they cook and they sing while they clean up, and the café does well even though people still always ask Dad why he doesn't do fish and chips.

'Make a fortune, Mr Patroclus, if you did fish and chips. I'm sure you could do a lovely fish in batter.'

My father's moustache, which is long and twirly, just droops when neighbours say this to him. 'I do moussaka, I stuff my tomatoes, I will not ever do fish with this batter.'

People like coming to the café all the same; I think it's because they like to hear my mum and dad sing, well maybe it's not quite the singing because their singing is terrible. And it's all Greek tunes that nobody knows and when they get carried away, which is most of the time, they stamp their feet and click their fingers which I, personally, find a bit rubbish. But the customers love it. The truth is, and I know you should never say this about your mum or dad, they're great. Except they just don't understand how terrible my school is.

'It is opportunity, Michael,' says Mum. 'Once in a lifetime. You must jump at it.'

'Yes! Of course you must jump,' says Dad. 'Jump like we jump.' And he claps his hands.

I give a shrug. I don't like to say no to them, I

really don't. I pick up the entry form we'd been given to show our parents. 'I'll see. Maybe they'll tell us something more about it tomorrow,' I say. But inside me all these warning lights are flashing on. Don't do it.

'Good boy.' Mum and Dad beam at me as if I had just turned into a saint or something.

I am about to turn off the TV when I hear the announcer saying, 'More jobs for Peasely, thanks to the new Blake Runner factory.' Then there's an interview with Mr Percival Blake senior who sounds dead posh and keeps saying 'Marvellous', except he pronounces the 'mar' as if he's a sheep: 'maa-maavellous. Peasely is 'maamaavellous' and his factory is 'maaaaaavellous' and it's maaamaaavellous to have so many people with no jobs so they can work in his factory. No wonder his son looks so dim; his dad has to be Mr Double Dim.

Except he then shows the camera the kind of runners his factory produces and they are...extreme. With a pair of Blake runners on his feet, a boy could burst the sound barrier and it occurs to me that at least Percy Blake junior has something with which to bribe Jaco and the Bins. A pair of Blake runners could save his life.

And I wouldn't mind a pair myself.

Chapter 5

The next morning I am out of the house early. See if I can get up the hill before Jaco and his mates.

I have the competition entry form in my pocket and I'm still worrying about it when I hear what's beginning to be a familiar voice calling my name: 'Patroclus. Wait!' She sounds as if she is way behind me.

I don't know what to think about Geek Girl. Half of me says keep away because she's trouble. She talks too much and the Bins have already binned her once; the next time they are bound to do something nasty. The other half of me says maybe, just for once, it really could be nice to have someone smart to talk to. So I stop and turn round, expecting to see her running to catch up.

And there she is just walking up the hill towards

me. Walking! 'Hey, if you want to catch someone, you run. Can't you run?'

'I can run very fast, Patroclus,' she says. 'I just don't like to.'

'And I'm Superman; I just don't like to tell anyone.'

She gives me a serious look. 'You're too small for Superman, Patroclus.' She's right there. Superman? Supermouse would be more like it. 'What are you going to do about the competition?' she asks. 'My mother wants me to enter it.'

'Mine too.'

'My parents think it's a chance in a lifetime.'

'Mine too.'

'Maybe we should go for it.'

We? I'm about to say, but I don't.

'Everyone else will,' she says. 'So perhaps it can't do much harm.'

She doesn't sound too convinced.

'Maybe not,' I say, but then I realise that's not what I should say at all. Of course, it's bound to do harm. And we – yes, we – should keep out of it. 'Don't enter. I don't like it.'

She nods, as if that was what she wanted me to say. 'You mean, trust first instincts.'

'Yes.'

And that is the exact moment that my right foot steps from the light into the dark, into the long shadow of the school. And I shiver, because I always do, every morning just at this point. Can't help it.

And there is Robestone at the gates. 'Early birds get the worms,' he says and gives a spiky laugh.

We trudge past him. At least the Geek has the sense to keep her mouth shut. It's best not to say good morning to any member of staff at Staleways, and certainly not to Robestone. Anything you say will be taken down and used in evidence against you.

Head down. Hands in pockets.

'Are we the birds or the worms?' the Geek mutters out of the corner of her mouth.

'You're not the first this morning, Patroclus,' he calls after us. 'Not the first worm.' And he laughs again.

What does he mean? I don't care, I'm on automatic pilot when I enter the main building. Left down the corridor, the Geek padding along behind me. Past the stairs that lead up to Sir Pent's apartment. Past classrooms 9A, 10A and then, right at the end, classroom 11, the endzone. Make it through the year and then that's it, I am out of here and free.

I push open the door, and then stop. For two whole years, every morning I'm first into the classroom. A little time of peace before the day begins. But today is different: for one thing, I have this new girl on my heels and, for another, Robestone was right: there's someone already here and sitting at the desk in front of mine. Percy Blake. Maybe his dad drove him in this morning after all.

He gives us both a cheery-but-dim smile. The Geek gives him a V for Victory sign which is weird: and then takes a desk in the front row, and begins to sort out her things. Books in a neat pile. Pencils out. A little bit of sharpening. Busy bee.

'Hallo,' he says to me. 'You were the boy who gave me back my glasses yesterday weren't you? Very decent of you.'

I shrug. 'No sweat.' He talks a bit like out of a comic. Who says 'decent', for heaven's sake!

He's giving his glasses a polish, the ones I returned. Then perches them on his nose. He really does look dim. I don't want to get into conversation with him but I can't help asking him about those specs of his. 'Tell me, why do you wear those things?'

'Desperately short-sighted. Glaucoma expedentialis. Very serious,' he says.

Who is he kidding? If there had been anyone else in the room I would have let it go but since it was the three of us and I didn't reckon that the Geek was paying attention and if she was I didn't think she would blab, I say: 'Blake, your eyes are fine. Those lenses are just glass, aren't they?'

'Oh gosh,' he says. 'You're a bit like Sherlock Holmes, aren't you?'

'Who?'

'A detective, Patroclus,' says the Geek without turning her head.

'A marvellous detective, actually,' says Blake. His 'ma-arvellous' sounds almost as sheep-like as his dad's.

'OK, but why the glasses, Blake?'

'I thought they made me look a bit more intelligent.'

I feel like saying, a bit more intelligent than what: Neil the no-brain nerd? But I just go, 'Oh.'

'Because I'm not that brainy really.'

'Oh,' I say again. Whoever would have guessed?

The Geek makes a sort of piggy snort, then blows her nose. And Blake grins. It's a bit more natural somehow than his dim smile, like there really is life inside the boy's brain after all, but then the grin slips back to the smile and he says, 'Daddy drove me into

39

school this morning. Did your daddy drive you?'

'No.' I think at this point I might have switched off. You know, clicked into school mode, but then the door swings open and in walks Jaco and a couple of his mates. I make a face at Blake that even a halfwit would recognise as 'shut up unless you want to get seriously bullied,' but it looks like poor old Blake doesn't even have the brains to be a halfwit because on he witters: 'It was the grey Jag. Do you have one of those? They really are maa-rvellous cars; mahogany dashboard. Do you know what mahogany is...?'

I can see Jaco's radar is twitching; even he can't believe this boy.

'Mahogany,' he says, all innocent. 'Ma-ho-gany? Do you mean: "my old granny"?'

Blake laughs. His laugh, if you can believe it, is worse than his smile in terms of dimness; it's a high-pitched titter that makes my nerves jangle, but Jaco only wolf-smiles.

'I watched your dad on the telly last night,' he says. 'His runners look all right.' Then he says it again, very deliberately. 'Look all right, know what I mean.'

I know what he means. This a golden opportunity for Blake to buy some serious protection. I can smell a deal a mile away. Jaco's message was loud and clear but one look at Blake tells me this boy is not receiving.

'Better than all right,' says Blake. 'The trouble is they're jolly expensive.'

Somehow Stef and Jaco are on either side of Blake's desk, their backs to me, like I don't exist, which I suppose is all right by me. Except I hate seeing them putting pressure on anyone, even someone like Blake.

'Oh,' says Jaco. 'Maybe there might be a bit of a discount for friends of the family.'

'Discount,' echoes Stef. Now *he* really does get the 'no genius' prize.

'Oh yes,' says Blake, 'Dad's always happy to do that for friends.'

A deal offer like this can only go two ways: good or terrible. To me, it's pretty obvious Blake's chosen 'terrible'.

'Well?' says Jaco, putting his hand on Blake's shoulder, and I know he's going to pull his ear, or pour something nasty down his neck, or tip his desk. And whatever it is will only be for starters. Welcome to the house of misery, Percy Blake.

'Well what?' says Blake, all innocently.

And I don't know what comes over me. Against

every rule in my book, I open my mouth. What an idiot I am. 'Why don't you just leave him alone, Jaco. He's not doing you any harm.'

Jaco turns round and blinks, like he's having trouble focusing on someone as small and insignificant as me. He thinks he is a great actor. 'What?' he says. 'What did you say, Trokka? Did you speak? Did you?'

That was it. I saw his boot swinging back. I saw Stef bunching his fist. I saw Maggot coming in through the door. 'Oh no,' I thought. 'Oh no.' and I tensed, waiting for the kick and the punch and the hands yanking me up and then my head being shoved down. So much for the free chips offer – that only worked if you didn't say boo to the goose.

And I just did.

Chapter 6

I would have ducked, dodged, run. Except I was stuck at my desk and they were standing.

I would have thought of something clever or funny to get myself out of it...

except...

...except, in that split second before the Bins really got to work on me, my mind froze.

But Jaco's boot doesn't thunk into my leg, and Stef's grimy hands don't yank me out of my seat.

There's a sudden loud, sharp bang, like a firework going off right there in the classroom, except – there's no smoke or smell.

'What...'

Stef flinches. Maggot gawps. Geek Girl looks startled and Jaco, mid-kick, swings round and hacks Stef instead of me. Stef yelps and then, because it was Jaco, he bites his lip and says nothing. Only Percy Blake seems unruffled. He's smiling, of course, and in his hands he is holding a Blake runner, white with a red lightning flash and thick see-through soles.

'Latest model,' he says. 'What do you think? Pretty marvellous.'

Jaco, his eyes fixed greedily on the runner, says, 'What was that noise? Sounded like a bomb going off,' but he doesn't sound as if he cares too much.

'Or a gun,' says Stef. He too is gazing at the runner.

Maggot points at Blake. 'It was him. I seen him do something.'

But Jaco is not really interested any more. It's the runner he wants. Blake hands it to him. 'It's my size,' he says, turning it round slowly in his hands. 'That's lucky, or what?'

I can't help studying Blake, he looks as dim as a five-watt lightbulb but he's got Jaco drooling. 'Don't 'spose you've got the other one, the one that goes with this.'

Blake gives his silly tittering laugh and I wince, but the Bins are too hooked to care. 'One shoe's not much good to anyone, unless you're Long John Silver, of course,' and he opens his desk and produces a second trainer.

'Who?'

'Pirate. Marvellous story, all about treasure...'

A couple more of the class come in and go to their desks. One of them is that cool customer with the waxy hair I noticed at the first lunch. He looks our way, interested by what's going on but smart enough not to butt in with questions.

'Can I try 'em?'

Jaco the wolf, asking? It's hard to believe.

'Of course, my father asked me to find a volunteer to try them out. If they fit, they're yours.'

Jaco kicks off his grubby trainers and shoves his feet into the gleaming-white new ones. 'They fit!'

'Oh good,' says Blake.

'Wicked,' says Jaco, bouncing up and down. He gives Stef a punch on the arm. 'Look!'

'Haven't got a second pair, have you?' says Stef, rubbing his arm.

'No, sorry, not here. Prototype, you see. Perhaps later.'

Jaco nods. 'Don't rush him, Stef. Blake's all right.' And he beams at the large, goofy new boy, like Blake was some favourite nephew of his and he was the kindly uncle.

I'm forgotten, for the moment anyhow.

But at least my brain has started working again. What was that bang? I look at the Geek and she looks back at me. Coincidence? Some fuse blowing? It couldn't have been Blake, could it? And this sudden appearance of the prototype runners, was that to save my neck? Because that is exactly what it did. And the runners fitted Jaco. A bit lucky...

He couldn't have known Jaco's foot size, could he? He was being so thick when Jaco was hinting, all that business of discounts and him not picking up on it and he had the runners all the time. I give Mr Percy Blake a good hard look, but it doesn't tell me anything: big, stupid and spoilt. A lucky coincidence then...

But the shoes fitting! I try to remember whether Blake had actually disappeared under the table at lunch yesterday but all I can picture is him bending down to pick something up. He couldn't have checked Jaco's foot size then, could he? No, that was ridiculous. Patroclus, you're losing your grip.

Chapter 7

'He could give me his.'

Stef is not happy. Of course he's not: one pair of Blake trainers that fit snug on Jaco's feet means that all the Bins are going to be jealous and want a pair too.

'Yeah,' says Maggot.

'What's that?' Jaco's pig eyes peel away from his footwear and turn on his mates.

'Why can't I have his trainers? New kids shouldn't have better gear than us.'

'Never have done,' mumbles Maggot in agreement.

Blake doesn't seem bothered by all the attention. He has his long legs stuck out from his desk and he's leaning back, looking round the room like he owns the place. He seems to notice the two swots who came in just a couple of moments ago. One of them's the waxy-haired new boy, Charlie Crocker. Blake gives them a wave and Charlie gives a quick smile and then turns back to the book he's taken out. Oops, not too good a move to be reading in public. Luckily the Bins' attention is all on Blake.

Stef is right about one thing: Blake's gear is much better than anything the rest of us have. Hadn't noticed because of his nerdy glasses and the dozy smile he has on his face most of the time, but his stuff is designer labels, everything. The kind of gear that singers on telly wear.

'Leave it out,' says Jaco. 'I said he was all right. Understand?'

Stef takes a step back and holds his hands palm out. 'No disrespect, Jaco.' The tips of his ears have gone deep red.

'None taken, old son.'

At that moment the lesson bell rings and the rest of the class stream in, including two more Bins, Joel and Henry Slinton, but I call them the Sullen Brothers. They sit behind Jaco and hardly ever open their mouths. No one talks except for Sally Ringfield and her little group, who ignore the rest of us. And Alex Frane, who is captain of the football eleven, and since even the Bins like to get into the team sometimes, he never gets picked on. He's so full of himself he doesn't need company, just a mirror. But sometimes he chats to the boy next to him, a skinny swot called Murphy, but only because Murphy helps him with his work. Nobody pays any attention to the new pupils, Blake, the Geek and Charlie Crocker, apart from Jaco and his mates of course. They are always keen to sniff out new victims. Everyone else knows the score: never get friendly with a new kid.

I know what you're thinking: but I didn't get friendly with Blake or the Geek. I just opened my mouth. Didn't mean to; it just happened.

Jaco gives Blake a pat on the shoulder. Friends for life, eh? Gives me the pig-stare that means I'm dead if I so much as step on his shadow and he slopes back to his desk, in the middle of the classroom, his two lieutenants going to the desks on either side of him.

And in comes Mr Dorner. He's old and so dusty he looks like he lives in the broom cupboard. But there's no real evil in him, if you know what I mean. He takes the register and then tells us to sit down.

We do.

And then something extraordinary happens. The class starts laughing out loud. I mean everyone in the class but Dorner, because his laughter muscles have gone dead, I expect, and the five Bins.

And what was the joke?

Not really a joke, more an accident, but what an accident. What a coincidence of an accident. You see, when we all sat down, three desks collapsed, and I mean really collapsed, every single separate bit came apart, and smacked to the ground with a crash. And the three toughest, don't-mess-with-us boys in the entire school are flat on their backsides, looking stunned and stupid. It is just the best thing I have ever seen.

Jaco is the first up and he is steaming. 'Who done this?' he shouts. I mean really shouts. But then he has to to make himself heard above the laughter.

'That'll do,' says Dorner, but Jaco ignores him.

'You better tell me who done this!' he shouts again.

Our laughter dies away and everybody finds something to look at that isn't Jaco. Stef is beetroot red in the face and has snatched up a desk leg and is holding it in his hand like a club, like he really wants to batter someone with it. He probably would, too.

'That'll do.' I've never heard Dorner raise his voice but he raises it now: 'Quiet!' and he bangs his fist on his desk.

And then the second most delicious thing happens: Dorner's big teacher's desk crashes apart just like the others did. I mean: Smash! And he's left standing there, his mouth gaping in a great round O, like a railway tunnel; and we're all in fits again. Whatever else happens, this is a good day, a day to remember. I grin like the rest of the class while Mr Dorner hurries out of the classroom.

All those desks going, a coincidence?

Not a chance. Some genius has snuck in here and set it all up. Someone who knows where the Bins sit. Someone in this class? The laughter dies away and everyone is thinking much the same as me I reckon, because we are all giving each other sneaky sideways looks. Can't be him, can't be him, can't be her.

And Jaco's doing the same thing too, eyeing us all, not looking so cross though because even he must have thought Dorner's desk collapsing was a bit of a laugh.

'Smile away,' says Jaco and he gives us a smile too but his pig eyes are black dots, 'but whoever done it, we're going to find him and when we do, there won't be too much laughing then. Believe me.' He goes and stands beside the desk in front of where his was, and just looks at the boy sitting there. The boy instantly gets up, and Jaco takes his place. Stef and

Maggot follow his example while the three deskless boys shuffle to the back of the class and then there is silence as we wait for Dorner to return with Sir Pent or maybe Mr Robestone.

Then this drawling voice says: 'Perhaps the perpetrator left a clue?'

I can hardly believe my ears. It's Blake. Doesn't he know when to shut up?

'Perpy what?' Jaco leans round to face him.

'Perpetrator,' says Blake, 'the person responsible. I just thought that if someone looked they might find a clue.'

'Like being a detective,' says Jaco sourly.

'That sort of thing.'

'Well you go and look then. You look and see what you can find.' He's not moving himself, of course: if Sir Pent has been called, anyone standing is likely to get sent straight to the Swotshop for a detention and that would just be for starters.

Blake stands up. 'OK,' he says.

'Sit down,' I hiss. There I go again, butting in when I should keep my mouth shut.

Jaco scowls at me. 'No one asked your advice, Trokka.'

Blake has his back to Jaco and the others. He closes one eye in a sleepy wink. Then he goes up to

52

Dorner's desk, gets down on his hands and knees, and sifts carefully through the pens, mark book, and sheets of paper scattered among the collapsed bits of the desk.

He stands up just as Sir Pent sweeps into the room followed by Dorner and Mr Robestone.

'Blake,' says the Serpent, his voice silky and dangerous, 'What exactly are you doing?'

'Trying to help, sir.'

'Oh? And how exactly are you helping?'

'Looking for clues, sir, and I found this,' and he holds out his hand, palm up. There's something tiny on it but I can't see. 'It looks like a flower, sir.'

'A flower. Are you by any chance, Blake, hoping to be funny?'

Blake looks puzzled. 'I don't think so. I was just saying what I found, that's all.'

Mr Dorner, who has gone across to Blake, picks the tiny flower out of his hand. He looks puzzled too.

'Well, Dorner, is it anything important? It is time we began our tests.'

'It's a flower, Headmaster, a little red flower, scarlet, actually. I think it's quite common but I don't know its name.' He looks up at Blake for a moment as if he is inclined to say something else but he doesn't.

Then Charlie Crocker puts up his hand.

'What is it, Crocker?'

'I think it's called a pimpernel, sir.'

Jaco turns round in his seat to stare at this swot who dares to speak out and know things about flowers. But then he, like the rest of us, is completely distracted by Blake, who gives one of his high tittering laughs. 'Pimpernel,' he says, 'isn't that ma-arvellous.'

Chapter 8

'I don't care,' says Sir Pent, 'if it is called deadly lampshade.' We hold our breath. He absentmindedly twists the showy gold bracelet he wears on his right wrist. 'Nightshade,' someone mutters from the front of the class.

The Serpent's hooded eyes flicker along the front row and rest on the Geek. It would have to be her, wouldn't it?

'Ah,' the Serpent exhales, 'new girl. What is your name, new girl? No, don't tell me.' He holds up a pale hand. 'I know everyone in my school: you're the Yabba girl, aren't you?'

'Minou Yabba.'

'Yabba Jabba,' sneers Stef so quietly only me, Maggot and Marco hear him. The Bins smirk.

'Yabba,' says the Serpent, as if the Geek hadn't

said anything at all. 'An unfortunate name but not one I shall forget.' He stares at her for a moment and she at least has the common sense to mumble something that sounds like 'I'm sorry for speaking' or squeaking, 'I couldn't hear properly', and then ducks her head. He turns his attention to the rest of us. 'Item one,' he says, 'unless the floriferous vandal owns up instantly there will be two from this class spending this Saturday in the Swotshop.' He waits for a moment with his arms folded and his long white fingers tapping impatiently. No one volunteers, of course. I expect most of us are wondering what floriferous means. 'Jackson!'

'Sir.' Jaco stands up.

'Select two for punishment.'

Jaco doesn't hesitate. He points at Yabba. 'Her, Sir.'

Sir Pent nods. 'Good choice, Jackson. And?'

Jaco turns and looks at me. He is not going to pick on me, is he, not when he gets free chips? 'And Patroclus, sir.' A whole day – a whole Saturday gone, just like that! So much for protection! I'll get my dad to put some rat poison in their chips this Friday. Knowing the Bins though they'll probably like the taste.

From the rest of the class there is a sigh. They're

in the clear. Look out for number one; that's the Staleways way. As for Prince Nerd, Lord of the designer trainer, he is staring up at the ceiling and humming to himself. Oh well, maybe he isn't so hopelessly dim after all; he's smart enough to keep his nose out of other people's bad business. Unlike yours truly.

'Very good, Jackson,' says Sir Pent. I swear that if we could see his eyeballs behind those tinted glasses he wears, they would be spinning round and round, hypnotising us all. 'Sit down.' We sit down with a plonk. 'Now that we have that bit of business out of the way, Mr Dorner, I think we can progress to item two. A little test, ladies and gentlemen, to make sure that everyone who should enter my competition, does so. We want the very best brains.' He rubs his pale hands together. 'Only the very best. There'll be exclusive invitations sent to those of you who do well today.'

I get the horrible feeling that he would like to scoop out those 'very best brains' and then nibble on them like they were some kind of special food. Somebody somewhere eats brains, I know that for a fact; my dad told me.

Sir Pent glances round the room to see if there is any objection to what he's just said. No one beeps, of course, though I bet everyone is thinking, why do we need a test? None of us likes tests because tests always mean that someone gets a detention, but since we never go through the tests afterwards to see how well or how badly we've done, we never understand why we're being punished. It probably means we've done badly but we just don't know. It's like a lottery except you don't get to win a million pounds but a Saturday Swotshop. And the detentions mean doing more and more tests. A whole Saturday doing tests, can you imagine? I'll tell you one thing though, although Jaco and his Bins do these tests, they never ever get sent to the Swotshop. See what I mean? Justice and Staleways have as much in common as roses and smelly socks.

'A test to find the best.' He smiles and rubs his dead-white hands together.

'Very good, Headmaster,' Mr Dorner says.

'Yes, well then. Carry on, Mr Dorner, and try to keep better order in here.'

'Of course, Headmaster.'

Sir Pent exits smoothly and silently on his crêpe-soled shoes and the door clicks shut behind him. Mr Dorner looks even greyer than usual; then he hands out the papers, and our pens scratch away for the next hour. We multiply and divide, and try to remember things about grammar. When the time is up, the papers are collected, and for the rest of the day we quietly grind through lessons and lunch.

'What's detention, Patroclus?'

I tried to find a seat by myself in the dining hall, but Geek Girl finds me and plonks her tray down on the other side of the table.

'It's better if we don't hang out together, Yabba.'

'Why? And you didn't answer my question.'

Since she's not going to budge, I tell her about detentions and the Swotshop.

'They can't lock you up for a whole day!'

I lean forward. 'They can do what they like, so we have to avoid getting picked on. Don't do anything. Don't get noticed. The best thing to be in this place,' I tell her, and I really mean it, 'is invisible.' I want her to understand because she's OK really, and smart – smart different, not smart alec, if you know what I mean. I look at the boy sitting next to her, forking his food into his mouth, his eyes down, and at the girl on the other side of him: pale, worried face and pigtails, and the boy next to her and the one next to him, and her and her. All the same, eyes down, scared. All you can hear is the mutter of low voices and the scraping of knives on plates. And the Bins, of course, you can hear them, throwing their weight around.

'You got noticed,' she says.

'I was stupid.'

Her eyes look huge behind her glasses. 'I don't think so.'

'Listen, once you get picked on, like we have, it means you keep getting picked on and if they keep seeing us together they'll keep picking on us.'

'Is that a rule?'

'Not one that's written down, but you can trust me.'

'Do you want me to move, then?'

But it's too late. Robestone is looking our way and pointing and here they come: Jaco, pig-faced because he hasn't had a chance to finish his lunch, and two of his gang, Stef, of course, and another one who's in a different class to us.

'All right Trokka and Trokka's weird-looking mate, off you go.'

'We haven't finished.'

Jaco looks puzzled. 'Well, I think you have, Trokka.' I feel hands grabbing me by my shoulders and as I do a slow vertical lift off the bench, Jaco leans across me, takes my plate and whips my fork out of my waving hand. 'Finished now,' he says through a thick mouthful of my shepherd's pie.

It is pointless to wish for some things, like being an extra two feet tall and having tree-trunk muscles, but it's no fun being dangled in the air by a pair of thugs, especially when the thugs are the same age as you. Of course a couple of tough mates would come in handy but who have I got? Geek Girl. But then to give credit where it's due, she's up on her feet, raging like a mad mongoose, spitting out insults, her glasses making her eyes look big and black like cannonballs.

'Drop him,' says Jaco, flushing just very slightly when she tells him he's a worm, a rag worm, 'and bin her.'

I am dumped and the poor old Geek finds herself upside down in the lunchroom bin, stick-like legs waving about for the second time in two days. Not a good record. The Bins laugh while Jaco takes his time finishing off my lunch. Finally, he puts down the plate and says, 'OK you can get her out now, Trokka. If you want to.'

I hesitate, just for a second because there's the little voice telling me about the rules I'm ignoring but I go ahead and ignore them anyhow. So I grab her waist and with half the lunchroom watching and the other half ignoring us because they've seen this sight too many times before and shepherd's pie is the one decent meal the kitchens can produce, I manage to haul her up and set her down on her feet.

She's got bits of bread and potato squished into her hair and her white shirt is stained. I feel sorry for her.

'Now,' says Jaco, 'follow me. Mr Pent wants to see you both.' And he spins round on his heels but the floor must have had a greasy spill on it because his feet shoot out from under him and he does a perfect Charlie Chaplin, arms windmilling so fast he looks like he's trying to take off and his feet are going backwards at the same speed. He keeps this up for about five seconds and then he falls flat smack on his face.

The hall goes very quiet, like the whole school is holding its breath. Someone at a table to the right of us shouts: 'One Bin down!'; someone else gives a whoop. Then a whole table the other side of the room begins to chant: 'Down! Down! Down!' They'll be for it...but maybe not, because just about everyone seems to be joining in, banging their plastic mugs on the table. Even the smallest kids. But it's not going to last because Robestone is striding towards us, his white pointy face looking furious.

Jaco, having scrambled to his feet, is now having

trouble keeping his balance. Maybe those fancy Blake trainers haven't got such a good grip after all. And down he goes again. Wonderful. But weird. No one else is falling over anywhere, but just where Jaco is I can see the floor has an oily sheen. A handy spill, what luck. A death patch, slippery as ice.

I grab Geek Girl's arm and tug her towards the door. It wouldn't do for anyone to think we were in some way responsible for this.

We slip into the corridor and I push the door to. The Geek has a wadge of paper napkins and is wiping her face and cleaning her specs with them. 'Where did you get those?'

'Crocker.'

'Really?'

'He was at the table behind us. Put them in my hand as we were going out.'

'Oh?' I push the door open a tiny bit. Charlie sees me peering in and, big surprise, gives me a thoughtful look. Blake's sitting beside him, tucking into his food, paying no attention to all the excitement going on. Then Blake looks up, spots me too and gives us such a big wink you'd think he'd been butted in the eye by a camel.

Giving paper napkins to someone who's been binned – that is not Staleways' style. I let the door close. Crocker couldn't have had anything to do with that slippery floor, could he? I'm half tempted to look through the door again just to see if he had some cooking oil stashed under his seat. But I don't because it is a ridiculous thought. How would he know what was going to happen? He wouldn't. How would anyone pinch one of those great big kitchen cans of cooking oil and smuggle it across a crowded room? They couldn't.

Geek Girl scrumples up the last of the napkins, looks around and then tosses them on to the floor. 'Pupils in the rubbish bins; rubbish on the floor,' she says briskly.

Two days and two binnings, but she's OK, no tears or nothing. 'Nice of Charlie Crocker to give them to you, the napkins.'

She gives me a funny look, 'He's different from the others, isn't he?' she says. 'Like you.'

'You're joking.'

'No I'm not. Like me, too. I'm different. You're clever, aren't you?'

'Used to be. Getting a detention on day two isn't so clever though. Come on, let's get this over with. I don't think we need to wait for the escort. That grease on the floor was a bit of luck, wasn't it? Poetic justice, if you ask me.'

I give her a glance because I don't expect her to know what poetic justice means. I only know because my dad is a big fan of poetic justice. My sister Pia is always complaining about this that and the other. Mainly about food. She is very fussy. Yesterday she complained that Greek yoghurt is smelly and has always gone bad before we get to eat it and why can't we have nice fruit yoghurt from Safeway's. And then she stomped off into the storeroom to fetch something and she knocked two dozen eggs off the shelf and they splattered all over her. My dad was delighted. 'This is it!' he shouted. 'This is what I am always telling you: poetic justice! You talk bad about my food and my food come and get you.'

There was a big row of course. Pia can shout as loud as my father and she was very cross because her white trousers were all eggy. I kept very quiet because I was the one who had stacked up the eggs on the shelf.

Geek Girl doesn't ask me to explain. 'Poetic justice,' she says. 'I like the sound of that.'

Chapter 9

'Well?'

We're on our own outside the hall and the Bins seem to have forgotten us. Twenty yards down the corridor is a set of stairs. Somewhere up the stairs is Sir Pent's lair. Never been there; never wanted to.

'Patroclus?'

I pull a face and bite my lip. I can usually make up my mind fast but it's like my thinking's got stuck; three options: wait for the Bins, go on our own, run. Three options. Round and round. Why? Because I have a bad feeling, that's why and if you have a bad feeling, you hide. I tell the Geek.

'I told you,' she says, 'I don't run.'

In my view running is handy. Talking is better of course. If you're a good talker you can duck and dodge and wiggle your way round most things. It should be a sport, like basketball. I see myself as being very good at basketball but I am too small and the only time I tried it I kept getting knocked over.

'Hide, then?' I suggest.

'I want to see the headmaster up close.'

'Why?'

She gives me a serious look and then shakes her head. 'I thought you were the smart one.'

'I am. My family is Greek. Greeks are always smart.'

'Then you should know that the most important thing is to know your enemy.'

I am impressed. I still don't want to go anywhere near him, of course, but she's right. If you know how the Serpent thinks then you can keep one step ahead of him and never get into trouble again.

'Lead the way, Patroclus.'

The stairs up to the Serpent's lair are narrow and badly lit and they twist right and they twist left and they go on and on and up and up, right up to the top floor.

There's the clattering sound of heavy feet coming down the stairs towards us. Bins. All of them with their red scarves round their right arms. They shove past us like we're nothing. 'Really pleased,' one of them is saying. 'He was really pleased, wasn't he?'

'Yeah, really...'

I hate the way they shove and don't see you. I hate their red scarves.

'Patroclus!'

'What?'

'Come on.'

She starts on up the stairs and I follow. Only one more flight, I think.

'The Pent House,' murmurs the Geek, when we come to a stop in front of a grey metal door blocking our way. There is nothing on the door, just two bulbs: one green, the other red. To the right of the door, up high in a shadowy corner, a CCTV camera peers down at us.

I give the door a knock. The green light glows and the door swings open and we are suddenly bathed in light.

'Come on, then. Come in.'

I don't know about the Geek but I can't see anything for a moment; I am just blinking into the light. I think of rabbits and headlights but the voice is the Serpent's all right and he sounds impatient.

His lair is huge and apart from the bright light shining at the doorway it is dim and green, more like it's underwater than underground, which is where I would expect his lair to be. Yes, he should be in a mouldering cellar, with fat dusty pipes to coil around. But how wrong can you be? Here we are, up in the Pent House and the place is glowing with soft green lights and more screens and gadgets than you could dream of in a thousand years.

'Don't stand by the door. Here.' We step out of the beam and finally see him down at the far end, behind a desk the size of a tennis court. 'Closer.' We move up to the desk and stand there together. In front of him there's a stack of papers that he's leafing through. Our test papers. 'I understood the prefects were going to bring you up here,' he says after a moment, briefly looking up at us. 'I don't like children wandering about my school unsupervised. What happened to them?' He's not really interested in us at all; his eyes keep flickering across to the bank of screens angled to the right of his desk.

The Geek is of course about to tell him, but I manage to give her a quick jab and she bites her lip. 'Don't know, Mr Pent,' I say. 'They told us to come and see you. I think they must have decided to have their lunch rather than climb up the stairs with us.'

'I see.' He makes a note and then does his reptile smile thing. 'Minou Yabba and Michael Patroclus,' he says, as though thinking out loud. 'How very foreign. Hmm. Good test papers, though.

Very good. Both of you. Unusual, that.' He sits back in his chair. 'Cheating, by any chance?' he asks encouragingly.

We shake our heads. He looks faintly disappointed. 'Clever, then. Clever people cause trouble.' He pauses and studies us. 'On the other hand, clever people make money and a school always needs money.' He is almost purring when he says this. Serpents don't purr though, do they. 'Money. Trouble or money, I wonder, which are you?' Then quite suddenly and in a different tone of voice, he says: 'Sitting behind the new boy, Blake, weren't you, Patroclus?'

'Yes, sir.'

He holds up another paper. 'His test was the worst in the year, so what do we make of that? Master Blake, heir to Blake's Runners, plenty of money there, wouldn't you say?'

I don't say anything because I don't think he is really talking to either the Geek or me.

'Plenty of money but not a lot of brains. Not like that other new boy, Crocker. He's in your class, isn't he? Brains and no money. How unjust the world is.' He smiles. 'But Mr Blake, now, there's plenty of money for the school there. You two, however, are a different kettle of fish. Are you going to make trouble for me; or are you going to make money?' His pale, heavily lidded eyes survey us and I can see the tip of his tongue running along his upper lip. 'And my competition, you will be entering my wonderful competition, I hope. Of course...' His voice trails away and his hands form a little steeple in front of his face as he looks at us.

I feel the Geek shift uncomfortably beside me. So much for knowing your enemy. I don't know what we are learning here at all, except that he seems to be thinking very hard about us.

'If we did well in the test,' the Geek says suddenly, 'does that mean we don't have detention?'

'Ah, she speaks. No, Yabba. It's the Swotshop for the pair of you. Clever pupils like my Swotshop. And I wouldn't want to undermine my prefects, would I? Don't worry, it won't stop you entering my competition. And I do think you should. Yes I do.' He nods thoughtfully. 'Parents are in favour of it of course.'

'Yes,' I say, 'mine are.'

'Of course they are. What a prize, eh? No one can resist a prize. And yours, Yabba. They too want you to enter?'

She shrugs.

'Of course they do. Enter and win, that's what I

advise. Enter and win. Off you go now but don't forget: Saturday morning, Swotshop one. I shall be keeping an eye on you two. And remember you either work with the school or the school,' he pauses, 'works against you. Back to your lessons.'

We turn and go and I quickly check out those screens he was watching the whole time. Monitors! Of course, he sits up here, spying on us all. Can't see everything though, otherwise he would have known what had happened in the hall.

Once the metal door softly clunks shut behind us the Geek gives a big shudder. 'He's disgusting!'

'Sh!' I point up at the CCTV.

'It's a camera,' she says. 'And I don't care if he can hear – *he* was threatening us! What does he mean, the school's going to work against us? And now he's spying – that's threatening too, isn't it. Well that is just not right.' Her chin is stuck out like she's challenging me to disagree with her. I can't; I don't even want to. She's got it in one. 'And I think,' she drops her voice to a whisper so she obviously doesn't want him to hear this bit, 'he's not human.' And she gives me a sharp look to see how I take this geeky thought.

I take it by pulling a face. 'What!' I mean I call him the Serpent because...because of his name and the way he is and anyway this whole place is a nightmare. But that doesn't mean to say he's a spooky blob from outer space!

But she's already on another tack. 'What are we going to do, Mr Clever Greek?' she says.

'Do the detention. Keep our heads down and stay out of trouble.' I start down the stairs.

'Are you serious?'

'Have you got a better plan?'

'I don't call that a plan.'

She's right, it's not. I don't really have plans, just my rules. That's the way it is with a nightmare; you can't plan your way out of it; you just have to get through it.

A Bin comes pounding up the stairs towards us. Jaco! He scowls but hustles past without saying anything. Did we get him in trouble? Here's hoping!

The Geek's not thinking about him though. 'What about the competition, Patroclus?' she says, once the Bin's out of earshot.

'Would you trust any prize that Sir Pent dreams up?'

'No way.'

'Me neither.'

'So we don't go for it; but some pupils will, won't they?'

'That's their lookout.' I'm a couple of steps below her; we're just walking down slowly, no hurry to get back into class, when she suddenly pinches my arm. Vicious, you know.

'You don't get it, do you?'

'Ow! Get what? Let go!'

She lets go but doesn't say sorry. 'He scares me, Patroclus.'

'I know.' I shrug. 'He's scary.'

She shakes her head. Impatient with me. 'He's bad,' she says. 'He's a bad man.'

We go down the last few steps into the cool, gloomy entrance hall. From the classroom corridor I can hear the murmur of lessons going on. I wonder if Pent is watching us from one of his cameras. I can't see one. 'Keep your voice down,' I say.

'This is war. Us against them.'

'Sh! *You* maybe,' I say, almost whispering now, 'not me.'

'Us,' she says firmly, squaring her shoulders and sticking her chin up again, like she's ready to pick a fight with any Bin who gets in her way, and sets off down the stairs ahead of me.

She'll learn, I think, as I follow her.

As it happens, of course, I am wrong.

Chapter 10

Swotshop.

It shouldn't be allowed. There shouldn't be anywhere in any school like this. But here it is, down in the school's basement; down the brown-walled stairway that you can only get to from the front hall; down to a long, badly lit corridor with a concrete floor and doors leading off to the left and right, all cellars or storerooms, I suppose. Swotshop is the first door you see as you come down the stairs. It's a heavy metal door, it makes me think of a door on a bank vault. It's orange with 'Swotshop' painted in big black letters across the top. It should have a skull and crossbones on it.

It is two minutes to nine o'clock. Me and the Geek and Timothy Tarker and Ben Porliss, both from our year, form a queue outside the door because we are not allowed in until the exact second of nine. Mr Robestone is on duty and he is a maniac for little details like that. We're not allowed to talk, of course.

Exactly on the hour, the door swings open and we file into the room. It's not like a classroom though there are desks and chairs all facing one way. For a start, there are no windows and one whole wall is made up of narrow drawers. Then each desk has a printer on it and an individual light angled down on it from the ceiling. Only our four desks are lit up. Weird. We are all sitting in little pools of light. It makes me feel like I am cut off. I can tell the Geek feels the same; she's looking around and drumming her fingertips on her desk.

Mr Robestone sits up at a high table, his face greenish from the light from a computer screen. 'Answer the questions on the sheet,' he says.

There is no sheet but before any of us can point out the obvious, Mr Robestone presses a button and the four printers on our four desks start to print, and out slides a test paper and we start work. As soon as we finish, about twenty minutes later, another test instantly prints out and we start on that. Every so often Mr Robestone gets up, collects the completed tests, and files them into the drawers on the wall. An hour passes. My hand is aching and my eyes are getting blurry. The questions begin to turn into a meaningless jumble of maths signs and problems about water in leaky pipes. A whole day of this!

The Geek puts up her hand and Mr Robestone looks up. 'I'm hungry,' she says. He looks back down. She tries again: 'I need to go to the bathroom.'

He looks up. 'Of course,' he says, 'but the rule is that if you interrupt a detention, it's doubled. Do you want to come here tomorrow, Yabba?'

She bows her head without answering and begins scratching away with her pen again.

The other two, Timothy and Ben, never stop working. Their heads are down, their shoulders hunched. They're the sort who always get picked on here. They've probably had loads of detentions before; they certainly seem to know the routine.

I sneak a look at my watch. 11 o'clock. Six more hours at least. I let my eyes close just to give them a rest and at that moment there is a banging on the metal door as if someone is attacking it with a sledgehammer. The whole room is juddering with the noise: it's like a war drum. Boom. Boom. Robestone looks like he's been stung by a wasp.

Perhaps this detention is wrong, illegal, and the police have come to arrest him. How good would that be?

He gives himself a juddering shake and then snaps, 'Keep working, you lot!' at us and then shouts, 'All right, I'm coming! Stop that din. Stop that din!' as he hurries to the door; but whoever is banging has no intention of stopping, or perhaps whoever it is cannot hear Mr Robestone. No windows. Metal door. Perhaps the room is sound-proof. You could lock someone away down here and forget about them and no one would hear them yelling; and I wonder if that has actually happened. Has anyone ever disappeared – lost without trace? I don't think so, but at least that's not going to happen to us.

Mr Robestone finally and angrily opens the door and the noise stops. 'Yes!' he snaps. 'Who are you and what do you want?'

'Gas,' says the stocky figure at the door. At least I think that's what he says. He is wearing a mask with breathing apparatus and is dressed in bulky blue overalls. It actually sounded a bit like 'mass'.

'What?'

'Mass!' and then there's a stream of rapid barking and burbling noises.

'Gas? I don't smell gas.' Robestone looks over his shoulder and sniffs at us with his splintery nose.

As he does, the overalled figure tilts up his mask and barks: 'Out! Everybody out!' and beckons us to do exactly what he says. I don't hesitate and nor does the Geek. The other two look bewildered.

'Stay where you are!' says Robestone. But he doesn't sound at all sure of himself now.

'Mo aighyar ents,' says the man, mask back in place but now separating each muffled word as if he were speaking to a brainless three-year-old. 'Hocked door. See!' He raps the door. Then, clearly angry now, he waves his arms around and spouts a stream of gibberish, mostly numbers, I think, that ends with something-'bites!'

'What *are* you talking about...?'

The man grabs Robestone by his lapels, obviously so angry he wants to shake him. I'm really hoping he will; I have never seen Robestone shaken before. It's almost worth being down in the Swotshop.

'Let go of me!'

He doesn't and the man gives him a thorough shaking. It's great. And while Robestone's now-blotchy red and white face flips backwards and forwards, our hated second master tries to say: 'Will you let me go,' but it comes out in little stuttering slices and is anyway drowned out by a further stream of furious, muffled barking.

With Robestone now so wobbly he can barely stand, the man tilts his mask again and very clearly says: 'Unless you vacate this building instantly, I shall call the police. You're in trouble anyway. Bylaw 16 and 17 flouted. Flouted. Do you hear!'

Meanwhile the Geek and I have edged up behind Mr Robestone but we can't get by because he is in the way.

'Gas!' I say. 'Gas, I can smell it!'

'What?' Robestone half turns, and the gasman reaches past him and grabs the Geek. 'If you don't mind, sir,' he says and shoves her out into the corridor and I nip out right on her heels. 'And the other two!'

Defeated, Mr Robestone stands out of the way. 'Detention over,' he says sullenly and our two fellow inmates jump up from their desks and dart through the door after us.

'Off ooh go. Quick as ooh can,' says the loud muffly voice of our gas man. That mask, now I see it close up, looks old and like one I have seen before somewhere, but I can't think where. The Geek and the others make off up the stairs but I hesitate for a second just to watch Robestone. I can't help it. I have never seen him like this. I don't expect anyone has. He's more rattled than my dad's van. The gas man says, 'Sign this,' and he shoves a clipboard under Robestone's spiky nose. Robestone signs the paper without even looking at it and then wipes his face with a handkerchief.

'How, exactly, how dangerous is it?'

The masked gasman waves his hands in the air. 'The doors!' he barks, 'Windows! Whole building. Big check. Top to bottom. Hurry!'

Not wanting to be overtaken by Robestone I sprint up the stairs. It'll take him all day to go round the building on his own and maybe with any luck, he'll miss a little window somewhere and the whole school will blow up. Oh bliss!

'Patroclus!' I can hear him giving an out-of-breath call but I pretend not to. He's not getting me to go round the school. 'Patroclus, come back!' No way.

Before swinging up the stairs I glance back and there's Robestone hurrying down the corridor, a massive bunch of keys in his hand. I hope there are a million doors down there and he has to unlock every single one. Good luck to him.

Just behind Robestone is the man in blue and

seeing me looking, he lifts his hand giving me a sort of 'hurry up and get out of here' wave, so that's what I do, taking the stairs two at a time and catching up with the Geek and the other two in the main entrance hall. Outside on the hill I can hear the 'Neenaaneenaa' of a fire engine.

The two boys look tense; Geek, though, is grinning.

'What should we do?' asks Timothy, glancing up the stairs that lead to the Pent House.

'Go home.'

'Perhaps we should complain,' says Ben. 'Gas leaks. They should close the school.'

'Maybe they will,' I say.

'I've a feeling they won't,' says the Geek. She's looking so smug, like she's just invented everlasting ice cream.

'Oh?'

'But I think maybe don't say anything,' she says to the other two. 'All right?'

'OK.'

The advice is good. 'She's right,' I say. 'Don't make a big deal of it to your parents. Just pretend nothing happened and with any luck we won't get done for only doing half our detention.'

The Neenaaneennaa-ing is loud now, like it's

right outside and when Timothy opens the front door, there's Peasely's fire engine nosed up against the front gate with firemen piling off, swinging open the gates, and running towards us. A small crowd of onlookers has already started to gather out on the pavement.

'Oh no, they're going to think we called them...'

I don't even have time to start thinking up excuses before they're running past us, telling us to leave the building instantly. The first two clop down the stairs towards the Swotshop; two more pound up to the first floor while yet more head back towards the kitchens. We make for the gate. Nobody's going to call us back now so we're in the clear. Fantastic.

I spot a few Staleways kids in the crowd, one or two of them with skateboards because the hill's quite hairy on a board, but mostly it's people I don't know. We sidle through and Ben and Timothy, looking distinctly more cheerful now, hurry off down towards town. The Geek and I follow them but taking our time. 'What do you think?' I say. 'Coincidence or what.'

'Coincidence! You're not that clever then, are you?'

'Meaning?'

'Meaning, didn't you notice. The mask.'

'Course I did. The gas mask, right.'

'Yes, but it was all wrong, wasn't it?'

I try to think back. It had looked odd – oddly familiar, that is.

'Second World War mask, for heaven's sake. How Mr Robestone didn't twig!'

'So the man was a fake.'

'Of course he was and he was there to rescue us wasn't he, why else? You're not such a clever Greek after all, are you?'

'Well who was he?'

'Same person who did the desks, of course.'

She could be right. A joker in the school. A practical joker – must be mad – someone like that in Staleways? But then things have been happening. And that little flower like a calling card. Crocker knew its name. I try to remember whether I noticed Charlie's face in that crowd by the gate, but I can't. Something's odd though. 'But the fire engine and all that. Don't tell me that someone from the school could fix that.'

She shrugs. 'A phone call. Someone called them. I reckon to stir things up a bit.' She claps her hands, delighted. 'It's not just us who don't like Sir Pent, Patroclus. We have an ally!'

At that moment we hear the sound of a car coming slowly down the hill behind us but instead of speeding up and passing us by, it rolls to a stop beside us. A smart black saloon with tinted windows so you can't see in. The rear window slides down and there, to my complete astonishment, is the king of all nerds, Percy Blake, 'Fancy a lift?' he drawls.

I can't help giving just a quick look round to see if anyone is likely to spot us. I mean I just have the feeling that hanging out with Blake can only get us into more trouble.

'OK,' says the Geek before I can think of a polite refusal.

'Your detention didn't seem terribly fair to me...'

Well spotted, Mr Blake.

'So I got Dad to drive up. Thought we could pick you up and offer you lunch. Would you like to come back for lunch? We'll drop you back afterwards. That detention does go on in the afternoon, doesn't it?'

'Well,' I begin to explain what happened but then he's off again.

'Oh how thoroughly spendido.' He claps his hands. 'There we are then, home for a feast.' He doesn't give us a chance to answer, just carries on. 'And this is my dad...' Oh well, I'm happy to be driven anywhere in a comfy car. 'Father, this is Minou Yabba and Michael Patroclus, the ones I told you about.'

Blake's father is the spitting image of him: the same dopey face, the same sticky-out ears, the same rather drawly voice. 'Delighted to meet you,' he says. 'Percy said you were his new friends. Blakes aren't awfully good at making friends, are they, Percy?'

'No, a bit hopeless really,' Blake says, sounding quite happy about this.

'Terrible hike up this hill every morning, isn't it?' says the father.

'You get used to it,' I say.

'Everybody just needs a good pair of Blake Runners, wouldn't you say, Father? Sprint up in jig time,' and father and son both laugh. Nothing particularly funny and their laugh is identical. Truly weird.

I catch the Geek's eye and raise my eyebrows. Lunch with weird losers, even if they seem pretty nice really? I don't know. 'Maybe if we could just have the lift, Mr Blake. My family might be worried if they hear the school closed and we were let out of the Swotshop early...'

'No problem at all,' says Mr Blake. 'Just give 'em

a call. What do you say, Minou?'

'Fine. Thank you very much. I'd love lunch.'

'And you, Michael Patroclus old chap, won't you change your mind? Mrs B would love to meet Percy's new chums.'

Oh well, what's to lose? And I suppose a part of me is curious to see what their home's like. Not that many people in Peasely own factories or drive cars like this one, and I don't think there can be many fathers and sons quite so odd and oddly the same as Blakes Senior and Junior. Bad luck to have inherited those ears and that laugh, too. 'Thank you,' I say. 'I'd like to come to lunch.'

'Good man!' says Mr Blake, jerkily accelerating away from a green light.

'Don't know anything about gas, do you, Blake?' says the Geek.

'Hardly know about anything at all,' he says, pressing his nose against the window and making goofy faces at the people outside who can't see him, 'except the family business.'

'You must know about runners,' I say, which, for no reason that I can understand, sends both father and son into peals of squiggly laughter again. I decide to keep my mouth shut but the Geek smiles and I have to say the laugh is funny, like a tickle, you know, that sort of makes you want to join in. And I find myself grinning too – after all, I have just escaped from the Swotshop – and that is a first.

Chapter 11

'Well, what do you think, Patroclus?' She's giving me a look like she thinks she knows that I know something. Those glasses can make her eyes look scarily big.

I don't know anything. 'About him? Them? The house? What?'

The Blakes live on the outskirts of town. Their house is hidden behind high walls and an electronic gate. It sounds flash but it's not really, just hidden. There is a gravel drive that sweeps in a curve up to and away from the front door and there is an old large white dog, a Labrador I think, that sleeps on the front doorstep and doesn't do much apart from lift its head when people come and go. Lunch with them was good fun: big pizzas in a big house – that has to be good. But now we're standing at the bus stop outside their house. They offered to drive us back but I don't feel so comfortable getting out of smart cars in front of our café.

'Him. All of them. You know. And this.' She digs her hand in her pocket and pulls out a squished little red flower and squints up her face at it. 'Found it in the field next to the house, when we were walking.'

I pick it out of the palm of her hand. 'It's the same as the one Charlie Crocker knew the name of, isn't it? I'm sure I've seen them around. Must be quite common.'

'You have?' She pulls a face. 'Didn't take you for someone who'd be interested in flowers.'

I'm not interested but I can't be bothered to start making protests. Instead I say: 'I like cooking too, so what?'

'So nothing. I just wondered whether you might know Blake from before.'

'Before what?'

'Before the beginning of term, you know, like old friends.'

'You're being weird. Do we seem like old friends? I don't know him any more than you, just from the start of term, a week.'

'OK. OK. I was just wondering. No need to get stressed. I'm only trying to work out who the mystery person is.'

'It's not me.'

'OK.' She looks back at the gates to their house. 'Do you think it could be him, then?'

'It could be anyone.' I'm thinking of Spiderman and stuff like that; it's always the shy, say-nothing sort of person who turns out to be the superhero. Most of the new kids have been so quiet, I couldn't even put names to faces, apart from Blake and Crocker, I suppose. But could our gasman rescuer be someone from the school? Caretaker? Cleaner? Cook? It doesn't seem likely.

'Interested in the school, weren't they?'

She is talking about the Blakes, and she's right. We were asked so many questions, particularly about Sir Pent, that it got to be like an interrogation. It was mainly Mr Blake doing the asking, but in such a bumbling, nice sort of way that you couldn't mind. Even Mrs Blake, who's French and kept wanting us to eat more, was pitching in. 'There is always a French Mrs Blake,' Mr Blake said and gave his high- pitched cackling laugh while Mrs Blake smiled and disappeared into the garden to prune the roses. 'Does it all the time,' Mr Blake said, 'cuts their heads off,' and laughed again. I mean that's not funny, is it? Sounds mad. But he can't be mad –

he has a brilliant business – but they are odd.

As for Blake, I can't make my mind up about him at all. Half the time he seems a bit like his dog: nice but not too many brain cells. And then you catch him looking at you, like he's trying to work something out. He wanted to hear all about the escape and laughed hysterically when I did my impersonation of the gasman shouting through his mask.

We didn't see much of the house, but Blake showed us the design room where there were stacks of drawings of different kinds of runners, all of them bristling with lead lines and little notes. There was a folder with TOP SECRET on it but he wouldn't let us look at that. 'Perhaps another time,' he said. I don't mind. I'm not that interested in runners though I wouldn't mind a pair of the really fancy ones. There was a room leading off the design office stuffed with chests, a big mirror and dressing table and loads of old clothes and make up and stuff. I thought perhaps it was Mrs Blake's dressing room. When Blake saw me peering he laughed and pulled the door shut. 'Just the old junk room,' and then we walked outside and he asked us about the competition.

'You're interested in it, then?' I said.

'Oh, very.'

'Have you entered?' asked the Geek.

'I'm not terribly good at competitions.'

'So why the interest?'

'I like to know what things are for, you know.' The Geek gave him a curious look.

'It's a scam,' I said.

He looked blank.

'A cheat. The headmaster, Pent, you know, he's got some scheme, I bet you, and it won't do us any good.'

'I think something bad will happen to everyone who enters,' she said.

I said I didn't think that was possible – there were going to be hundreds entering.

'The winners, then,' she said. 'You wait. I've got a feeling.'

Blake blinked slowly like he was trying to work something out, then he suddenly asked: 'Tell me what you had to do for your detention.'

We described the Swotshop to him: the room, shelves, the endless test questions that clacked out of the printers.

'And what was the point?' he said.

'No point, Blake,' I told him. 'You've got to get it into your head, nothing at Staleways has a point;

it's pointless. What you have to do is...'

'What?'

I hesitated because I'm not sure that I want to tell him anything personal, so I just shrugged. 'Be invisible,' I said, 'that's the best thing.'

'It's Patroclus's thing,' said the Geek. 'He told me to be invisible too. He's a bit weird, isn't he?'

Blake laughed and then we just fell to talking about other stuff. Blake seemed a tiny bit different then, not unfriendly or anything but like the lights were out, if you know what I mean. Dim. He could get a leading role in that old movie, *Clueless*, and I wondered just how reliable he was, especially when he told us about Sir Pent and how he had been to their house for dinner. Can you imagine? Apparently he wanted them to sponsor the competition but he didn't know if his parents had agreed or not. Didn't seem bothered.

I don't think Blake would deliberately dump us in it, but maybe without thinking he'd blurt something to Jaco about some of the stuff we said over lunch. Me and the Geek don't want any more bad publicity, thank you very much. So when he told us about Sir Pent being a favoured guest, I decided it was time to go. The Geek stood up and said she would come too.

I don't think I'll be coming back, either. Nice as Blake is, I don't think I need to keep company with some odd rich boy who believes Sir Pent is 'not that bad'.

The bus comes and the Geek and I don't talk much on the journey home. She's got her forehead up against the window, staring at the dull houses and then as we come bumping into the centre, she says: 'It would be good though, wouldn't it, to be able to rescue someone from detention. Don't you think it would be cool, dressing up like the gasman, giving Mr Robestone a fright?'

'If we dressed up in that boiler suit,' I said, 'we'd look stupid. We're too small. I suppose he might think he was being attacked by blue midgets and faint.'

'You rescued me, Patroclus, twice.'

'I lifted you out of a dustbin; it's not the same thing.'

She gets off the stop before me. 'Meet you tomorrow?' she says.

'Tomorrow's Sunday.'

'That's what I mean. Just how clever are you, Patroclus? OK, OK. Only joking. See you tomorrow, yeah?'

'OK.'

She gives a wave and a grin and bumps into an

old woman because she's not looking where she's going and then she's off the bus and skipping down the street. She's all right, Minou Yabba, with her frizzed-out hair and giant glasses; she may be a geek, *the* Geek, but she's the clever one, not like Blake; and she's quite funny really.

I am thinking these thoughts and feeling good as I head down my street. I'm just not paying attention and paying attention is one of my rules.

'Trokka, what a surprise.'

It's Jaco and maybe half a dozen Bins, all with their red bandanas, hanging round the entrance to our café. What are they doing here? They don't come round on Saturdays. My dad is standing in the doorway, and he's got that look he has when he's trying to hold on to his temper.

'Michael, you tell these boys, they come Friday I give them chips how they like, but not Saturday. One day a week is all.'

'Michael,' oozes Jaco in a pretend friendly voice – he's not the world's greatest actor, Jaco, but then he doesn't have to be. 'Michael, you tell your dad that we'll come round whenever we like, 'cause we just love his Greek chips.'

'Uh!' my father throws his hands in the air.

'You broke the agreement,' I say. 'You got me put

in detention for no reason.'

'Trokka, this is a new school year. There *are* no agreements. It's time for re-negotiation, isn't that right, Stef?'

'Yeah,' says Stef. 'The very word, renegosherhim, Jaco. He were the one put the skids under you, I bet.'

'Did you, Trokka, my son, did you put the skids under me, at lunchtime yesterday?'

'What are you talking about? How could I have done anything? There was something spilt on the floor, that was all. Come on, it was an accident.'

'And before that, when I fell over and got lunch on my face,' says Stef.

'And the famous collapsing desks, Trokka. Was that your little bit of wizardry my son?'

'No. I don't know how to collapse desks.'

'Coincidences then, eh, Trokka?'

'And what did you and the weird girl say to Pent when you were up there? Eh? Been stirring it, Trokka?'

I don't answer that.

'And this, Trokka.' Jaco folds open a bit of paper and thrusts it in my face. 'What about this little fancy flower. You a bit of an artist, Trokka – a little bit of – what did he call it, a pimpy nell.' The Bins laugh, but no one's making jokes. I'm having to tilt my head back because he's almost shoving that bit of paper in my mouth.

'But you can write, can't you, and you can read.'

I can see what it says: 'Be warned, Jaco. The Pimpernel will deal with bullies...'

'Is this you, then, Trokka?'

'No.'

'Do you know who it is?'

'No.'

'Well, if you find out, it would pay you to tell me. Until then, I think we'd like our chips, Trokka. Chips with everything, right?'

'Dad, would you get them some chips?'

'Yes. Yes. Yes. I get some chips. And you,' he says, pointing his finger at Jaco, who smiles innocently back at him, 'you big boy, you leave my boy alone. You understand me.'

'Of course, Mr Patroclus. We have very good understanding skills, that's why Mr Pent made us prefects. It looks like you have good understanding skills too.'

My father doesn't reply to this but he mutters under his breath while serving up the chips in little white bags.

'Ta, Mr P,' says Jaco when they all have their portions and then he and the gang saunter off down the street. 'Bye now, Trokka, see you Monday. Keep your nose clean, and no more funny things happening, eh? Cheerio!' And they're gone, six of them walking abreast down the middle of the street.

'They think they are cowboys,' says my father dismissively. 'And you, Michael, what bad things have you done to bring them here? What do I tell you? I tell you to be good.'

'I am good. It's the school. I've told you about it, Dad. It's a terrible school...'

My father doesn't listen. 'Michael, what do you know? It is a beacon, this school. It gets much funds, much money. We are very lucky to have this school here. You are a child; you cannot judge these things.' He wags his finger at me. 'And now Mr Pent has this competition. You go in for this competition, Michael. It will be a very good thing. And you keep away from these boys.'

'They're prefects, Dad. I can't keep away from them. They pick on us.'

'Then you learn to be very smart, Michael.' He pats my cheek which he does when he feels affectionate. I don't mind but his hands are oniony. 'You're a clever boy. You work hard and you can be a big businessman like me. We make a chain of Patroclus cafés.'

'Very good, Dad. Do you want me to help serve tonight?'

'Sure. Tonight we are busy.'

'You don't need me now?'

'No, no. I will call you.'

'Dad, what's a pimpernel?'

He pulls a face. 'It is a spot, no?'

'It's a flower.'

He shrugs. 'Why you ask me then? What do I know of flowers, Michael. I cook meat. Ask your mother.'

But neither my mother nor my sister are around. I go to my room and log on to the Internet and do some research and then I grab my bike and cycle to the library. I get there about ten minutes before closing but I manage to find what I'm looking for.

That night, when the last customer has gone home and we finish tidying and washing up, Mum and Dad sing together. They always do. My sister, Pia, she loves the singing too; I think it is terrible. The songs are so long and they are all in Greek of course; and they are about such crazy things. I mean the one that had my dad in tears was about a beautiful goat that lives on an island. Can you believe that! But this is my family.

We watch the news. There's something about Sir

Pent's competition. Some excited pupils from the next town are interviewed and asked about their chances. They are convinced they are going to win of course. They think the competition is fantastic and Mr Pent must be the best headmaster in the whole country. What do they know! The deadline for all entries is tonight. At midnight. Four hours away and the winners will be announced at the end of Monday. Barely forty-eight hours and they'll be off on the cruise of a lifetime. That's if you believe Sir Pent.

I slip away before my father asks me yet again if I have entered. He'll explode if he ever finds out I that I tore up the entry form and questionnaire the day they arrived.

Up in my room, I get out the two books from the library and I read and read and my mind is buzzing like a beehive. The Scarlet Pimpernel, not just a plant but a superhero! Is he fact or is he fiction? Cooler than Spiderman though, and that's a fact. I read until I can't keep my eyes open any longer. I want to phone the Geek and tell her what I've found out, but it is too late. Tomorrow though, it can wait till tomorrow. My last thought before I fall asleep is, do I tell Jaco? It just slides in to my head. Maybe he would leave me alone. Invisible.

Chapter 12

'You mean I was right?'

The Geek was round my place about ten minutes after I phoned her, and she was so fidgety I could hardly get her to listen while I was telling her what I found out about the Pimpernel.

'Yes. Sort of. Except you thought it was Blake.'

'And you don't?'

'Of course I don't. You were there, you saw what he was like; and then you've got Sir Pent being all matey with the family...'

'So it's just a story,' she says flatly.

'Yes, that's what I'm telling you. It is a story but listen, it's much more than that. The Pimpernel, it's his code name and the flower is his mark – like a sign to his enemies – so it really gets under their skin when he's outwitted them. He's really, really smart and no one knows who he is apart from his trusted friends; and it's at the time of the French Revolution when they were killing loads of aristocrats, whole families. The Terror, it was called. And he used disguises and that, and though they hunted him, the French police could never get him.' I'm excited, I know I am; I'm kind of rattling out everything I found out but probably not making a huge lot of sense.

'So the gasman was him, in disguise, is that what you're saying; someone who thinks he's this bloke from your story?'

'I don't know, but we got rescued, didn't we? And things have been happening at the school, little things. But I tell you, nothing ever happened like this before, not at Staleways; not in all the time I've been there; nothing that made the prefects or Mr Robestone look so stupid. It's like someone is waging a campaign. You know what I mean?'

'You don't think it was coincidence after all? That was what you were trying to tell me yesterday, wasn't it?'

'You want me to say you were right and I was wrong, is that it?'

'Yes.'

Smug or what! But still fidgety. 'OK! You were

right. Satisfied now?'

'Who is it then?' she says. 'If it's not Blake, who?'

'Someone who knows the story.'

She claps her hands. 'Charlie Crocker!'

I've wondered about him, too. 'Could be. Bit small. But he's smart.'

'And always in the right place when things happen.' She pulls a face. 'Doesn't seem very brave though, does he?'

Who does? But I know what she means. So I say: 'OK, so we don't know yet but we watch. Little things. It doesn't have to be someone in our class but it's likely to be someone new...'

'Not necessarily,' she says. 'Could be someone who's fed up with the school and the way the Bins just bully who they like. Someone who was on the spot when all those things happened. And as you said, someone who knows the story... Anyone come to mind?' She's looking at me like she thinks I'm hiding something, which is a bit rich given I've done all the finding out and have been up half the night reading all this stuff.

'No, not yet.'

'I know.'

'Who?'

She claps her hands again. 'You, of course.'

'What! You can't be serious! How can it be me? That's just stupid. How can I rescue myself? Yeah? How about that!'

'You could have a gang. In the story, doesn't he have a gang? Isn't that what you just said?'

'Yes, but do I have a gang? Have you seen me with anyone, other than you?'

'No, but who knows about the story? You do.'

I throw my hands up in the air in exasperation - it's like my dad, I know, I can't help it. Maybe it's a Greek thing. 'It's a story! Anyone can read a story! And listen...' I tell her about what happened with Jaco and the Bins last night. 'If I was this smart character would I let them push me and my dad around like that? No way.'

She shrugs. 'OK then. Do you want to join whoever this person is, make a gang, like in the story?' She doesn't wait for me to answer. 'I do. Unless it's a stupid boy thing and he doesn't want girls.'

She gives me another one of those looks like something is my fault but I ignore this, because I am thinking about what she has just said. With all the buzz of finding out about the Pimpernel, and reckoning that there really is someone like him in the school, I hadn't thought about doing anything more than trying to work out who it was. She's right, of course: what's the point of doing that unless we can join in and help. Us against them. But that would mean ditching one of my rules and stepping into the spotlight, wouldn't it? Except maybe not – nobody keeps much more hidden than the Pimpernel.

'OK, yes. Why not?' And then I think a bit more about the school and less about me and my rules. The whole school is wrong, bad, a cheat; and it's not right that Jaco and boys like him get used to terrorising anyone they want to. It's just not right. 'Yes,' I say more firmly, 'Definitely.'

'Good. Something is going to happen, Patroclus. I can feel it in my bones. I can feel it but I just don't know what it's going to be!' She has both her hands up, gripping her wiry hair, tugging at it, as if somehow she could pull answers out of her head. 'It's the competition. I just don't get it.'

'To catch clever students?'

'But why?'

'So he can use them in some way.'

'What way?'

'I don't know.'

'It doesn't make sense. If he wanted to catch clever students, why send them off on a cruise?'

'Why do you expect it to make sense?' I say.

'Maybe it'll be like a floating workshop. Not just Saturday detention but a whole year. Think about that!'

She pulls a face like she's tasting the idea and it tastes like school cabbage. 'Better not send in your entry form then, Mr So Clever Patroclus.'

'I didn't.'

She grins suddenly. 'Me neither.' Then: 'What do we do now?'

'We watch. We wait. We find out who the Pimpernel is.'

'Unmask this person?'

'No! Of course not. We get a message to the Pimpernel and then we make a plan.'

'A trap for Sir Pent, so he can't do whatever terrible thing he's planning to do with the winners.'

She's catching on.

Chapter 13

Day one.

We watch. But we don't have to wait long.

I'm up extra early for school and then I walk fast. Eyes on the pavement, head full of plans. Spies. That's what we are: spies. Watchers. But it's not just the Pimpernel we need to find; we need to find a way of spying on the headmaster himself. Catch him red-handed cheating or stealing or lying. It doesn't matter what. Just catch him and then let the papers and the television reporters drive him right out of Peasely. That would do it. Then maybe we could get someone decent to run the school.

Head down. Shoulders hunched. Up the hill and through the gate so quick I'm like a shadow. Mr Robestone blinks with surprise but I'm gone before he can give me his usual sneer.

Yes! First into the classroom just as the cleaners are going out. No Percy Blake this time. Cleaners! I dump my things and dash back into the corridor just in time to see two blue-coated figures turning down towards the kitchens. Only glimpsed them but I'm sure they were both women so neither of them could have been the gasman – could be in league, though. I make a note to find out all about the cleaners. I have to keep my eyes peeled and miss nothing.

I go back into the classroom. Still time to get my things sorted. I open my desk to stack in my books for the day.

And there's a message in blood red on the inside of the lid.

I get such a shock that even though I know I'm on my own I can't help spinning round to check there's no one standing behind me. No one. Of course not. I let out my breath and turn back, half expecting it not to be there, but there it is: red spiky capitals and a squiggly little flower. A message from the Pimpernel!

DON'T BE SMART!

That's what it said and with an exclamation mark

too. A threat. Like: Butt out! or Mind your own business! Who was it? And how did whoever it was know what me and the Geek had been planning? Who knew about the Pimpernel but me and the Geek? I told her; and she wasn't the Pimpernel, and nor was I. We're the watchers and we're being watched. Creepy.

I stack my books inside the desk.

But maybe it wasn't meant to be a threat; maybe it's more like: Don't get noticed. Keep quiet.

I lower the lid quickly as the others start to drift in. I can feel that the tips of my ears are still burning. I busy myself with things. No one talks. It's the usual morning gloom. Apart from one thing – when Charlie Crocker comes in, he gives me a quick grin and as he drifts by my desk murmurs: 'Heard about Saturday – glad you both got out of that detention.'

'Thanks.' No Bins in the room yet but people listen even when they pretend not to, pass on bits of gossip, maybe keep themselves safe. I busy myself with my things but out of the corner of my eye I watch Charlie Crocker go over to his desk and when he thinks no one is paying attention he slides a book out of his bag, folds it into a comic and calmly starts to read. He doesn't give away much, that one. But he's not stupid. I liked the way he hid his book, shows he learns quickly; Jaco would slaughter a new kid for being a reader. Keeps to himself too. One to watch, then.

Carefully I open my text book. Invention number one. A piece of broken mirror that I filed into a square about the size of a postage stamp and stuck onto the inside cover. By tilting the book a little I can check out all the rows behind me without turning round. It works well.

Who else? Who's to say the Pimpernel isn't more than one person? That means I shouldn't leave out the girls. How about Sally; she's got a mouth and stands up for herself but she and her mates keep to themselves, a little clique. She's not interested in us mice. I can't see her rescuing anyone from anything. Alex, back right-hand corner, has got half the juniors as his fan club but having a fan club doesn't make you a hero. He's too vain anyway, always checking his hair or...there he goes, dabbing at a little blond spike with his comb.

Then there's the rest of us: mice, grey, never looking anyone in the eye, keeping out of trouble: rows of us and not one a hero. But isn't that the point about the Pimpernel; he doesn't look like a hero at all, ever. I take another look. Simon Merry, a quiet little swot sitting in the row behind me. Him? He's not so different to Crocker; not so different to the Geek or to me, for that matter, and there's spoilt-boy Blake with the sticky-out ears... Will the real Pimpernel please stand up and wave a flag? I just don't think anyone from in here could be him or maybe her.

Back to the idea of a cleaner, then. Who else could get in and out of the classrooms when they were empty and have the time to rig up those booby-trapped desks the other day, or leave my message? Or carry out that weird rescue from the Swotshop. It sort of makes more sense. But then why would a cleaner risk losing their job to help out the odd pupil? They might just hate the school of course, like the rest of us; but cleaners are free, freer than us; they can leave, maybe get a job somewhere else.

I'm going round and round and circles. It's still a couple of minutes before the bell for first lesson. Neither Jaco nor Stef are here yet; they're usually last of course. And Percy Blake's desk in front of mine is still empty.

The Geek's up at the front rummaging in her little shoulder bag, not looking my way, pretending I don't exist.

I am waiting for her to open her desk but she's sharpening pencils now and arranging them in a little plastic pen case. Come on! At last. She opens her desk and then, just like I did, stares at it for a half second and then quickly lowers it. She looks sort of stiff, then she slowly half turns and looks my way, doesn't say anything but I can tell she wants me to know that she has to tell me something, and I don't have to be a genius to know what it is.

Since there's no way of passing notes in class, I pick up one of my pencils and snap it in half. Break. Get it? She turns away without giving any sign that she's noticed my signal or not. At that moment Mr Dorner walks in and we all stand up.

'I saw that, Patroclus,' he says. 'Damaging school property.'

'It was one of my pencils, Sir, and it was an accident.'

'Black mark.'

No point in arguing and drawing more attention to myself. Three black marks and I'll be back in the Swotshop.

Dorner picks up a thickly typed sheet from his desk. 'New rules,' he says. Beginning of term there are always new rules to add to the old rules. 'Anything that gets broken,' drones Mr Dorner, 'or damaged and that includes, pens, books, desks - black mark instantly.' He gives a slight cough and carries on with the list of more things we are not allowed to do: no contact with pupils from other schools; no communication whatsoever with local newspapers; meal and breaktimes no mixing with pupils from a different class... Where's this one come from? The competition? What does he want? For us to be gagged, to wear muzzles? No one to question anything. I stop listening. What's the point? Nothing's allowed anyhow and in this prison we've got punishments coming out of our ears, and half the time we don't know what for. Except I do know what for, it's all to keep us like mice - obedient and frightened.

At last he finishes, we all sit down and the lesson begins. Then about two minutes later, Maggot and Stef with his crooked rat's teeth stroll in. Stef clips Simon Merry round the back of the head. Mr Dorner pretends not to see and Stef says 'Sorry' in that sneery way that bullies have, just so that they can draw attention to what they have done. Merry says nothing of course, though a couple of minutes later I see him rubbing his head. I bet Stef knuckled him and that really hurts.

I keep quiet. But I see what happens. I see it all.

'Don't be smart' says the message underneath my desk lid and I won't, not now. But I'll do something later. I don't know what it is yet, but Stef and all the other Bins are going to pay. They really are.

A moment later in comes Jaco, and who is with him? Mr Percy Blake! What a surprise. And it's like they're best mates. 'Blake was seeing the headmaster, sir.'

Well, well. Jaco is even doing Blake's speaking for him.

'And I was told to accompany him.'

'Yes, all right,' says Dorner. 'We've already started so please sit and open your books at page 56.'

Jaco doesn't sit down and open his book. 'Headmaster thinks we got a trouble-maker in the school,' he says. 'Someone leaving stupid notes.'

'What notes, Jackson?'

Jaco knows we're all watching him, waiting – 'Stupid notes, Sir, with that flower on 'em. Head doesn't want them. Promises a reward for any information.' He turns towards us. 'No one got anything to tell your old mate Jaco?' he sneers.

Blake's looking round too, like he's suddenly been elected deputy sheriff. It'd make you spit except he looks such a phoney.

'No?' says Jaco. 'How about you, Crocker?'

'How about me, what?' says Charlie evenly.

Jaco smiles. '"How about me, what?" Very good, but I'll tell you what, me-what Crocker, anyone caught having anything to do with our clever Mr Pimpy, the note writer, is going to wish he'd never been born. The Head wants us to ask a few questions and you know what, Crocker, we'll start with you. Break time. All right?' He puts on a pretend frightened expression. 'Ooh,' he says, 'maybe Mr Pimpy will come and rescue you. Wouldn't that be scary for us...I don't think.' He gives us all a nasty look and nobody says anything, even Sally holds her tongue. What is there to say? We all know what's going to happen: Crocker's going to get mashed – unless we do something.

'Thank you Jackson, perhaps you can sit down now.' I reckon Dorner doesn't like Jaco, but Jaco doesn't give a fig.

'Thank you, Sir.'

Jaco sits down, leaving Blake still standing, his eyes narrowed, thumbs hooked into his belt, head nodding. I know! I've got it, he's trying to be that cowboy actor. Clint something or other. What a dozer!

'You can sit down too, Blake.'

'Oh sorry, Sir!' says Blake, giving a little jump, like

he'd forgotten what he was meant to be doing! 'And I'm so sorry to be late. In fact I always try to be early.'

He's off the wall! No one says things like that. But Jaco is smiling at him like he's Blake's friendly old uncle. It's enough to make you want to throw up.

'Thank you, Blake.'

Blake plonks his things on to his desk. 'Hello, Patroclus,' he whispers.

I don't make the mistake of answering him as I can see Dorner looking in our direction. Anyway I am not sure I want to have anything to do with someone who has Jaco for a bodyguard.

A moment later, Crocker yelps and clutches his left ear. A pellet. And Stef is grinning. 'Mr Dorner,' says Crocker, jumping to his feet, but it doesn't do him any good because Dorner just gives him a black mark for getting up out of his seat without permission. Crocker slowly sits back down but he turns and gives Stef a look, no expression on his face. It's just a look but the Bins are going to count it as asking for trouble. Sure enough Stef gives his rat smile. I didn't think Crocker would be someone who would get himself into the firing line like this. The Pimpernel doesn't draw attention to himself, not to his real self. Someone has to tell Crocker how to deal with the Bins – and then of course I realise, it's me. I'll have to. There goes another of my old rules.

And so the lesson goes on. After a while I see Blake's head tip forward and his breathing seems to get a little louder. Then I hear him snore, just once, very quietly. Asleep! That's one way of getting through the day. I can't help being impressed. Five minutes before the break bell goes, he lifts his hand and asks permission to go to the lavatory. Normally this is not allowed but Blake seems to have some special deal and off he goes.

Jaco gets up first and stands by the door. 'Crocker,' he says. 'Back here at five to. Don't make us come looking for you.' Then he and the other Bins file out, Stef carefully adjusting the red bandana on his arm. The rest of us follow. Crocker doesn't move though – I see him taking out his book, not bothering with the comic this time. He smoothes down the pages and starts to read. He's a cool one.

I head for the yard where the younger pupils like to kick a ball around in their free time. All the seniors will be down by the kitchen, buying snacks. And the Bins will be there too, sharks cruising around taking what they want.

I go over to the tall black iron fence and gaze down towards the town, which is washed in milky winter sunlight. A moment later the Geek's beside me.

'What are we going to do?' she says.

'I don't know. It's a trap, isn't it? Jaco reckons the Pimpernel will have to show himself and they'll get him - and if he doesn't they'll beat up Crocker anyway.'

'We have to do something.'

I make a face. 'Didn't you get a message too?'

'You mean 'don't be smart'? Was it you?'

'No. How many times have I got to tell you?'

'Were you in first?'

'Yes.'

'Well, then.'

'I'm not the Pimpernel.'

'Pity.'

Yes, maybe.

'What about Crocker, could he be?'

'Only one way to find out,' I say. 'We have to be back at five to. If the Pimpernel is in the school, he'll turn up. He rescued us, didn't he? And if no gasman comes bursting in then maybe we'll see Charlie getting out of a fix and then we'll know he's the

Pimpernel.'

'And if neither of those things happen?'

I don't feel very brave but I know this is it, it's time to make a stand. 'Then we do something,' I say.

'Yes. I knew you'd have a plan. What is it? To charge in screaming.' She grins.

'How did you guess?'

'You told me Greeks were very cunning.'

I look at my watch. Six minutes to go.

A ball thunks into the fence above my head. Time to go. I feel a hard knot in my stomach. The Geek doesn't seem bothered though; I think she'd happily charge an army of Bins.

We turn away from the fence and then to our surprise we see Blake over the other side of the yard, talking to a first former and the first former is pointing his hand towards the far end of the main building. Blake gives the first former something, a chocolate bar maybe, and then hurries off in the direction he'd been shown.

'Where would that take him?'

'Round the back of the kitchens.'

'Isn't that a long way round?'

'Yes.'

'Can he get back in there?'

'Yes, but you're not allowed to go through the

kitchens.'

'Odd.'

'Very.'

We run back into the building and have to shove our way through a small crowd out in the corridor by the classroom. Word's got around. And we're a minute late. There's shouting coming from inside the room. And Bin laughter.

'Good at drawing flowers, are you?'

'Know about Mr Pimpy?'

Through the glass panes I can see a bunch of them around Crocker, shoving him backwards and forwards. First Stef, of course, with his back to me, and then when Crocker staggers off balance, Maggot on the other side gives him a barge, so he goes lurching forward again. Crocker's face is a mask. Hard to keep your cool when you're being battered about like a basketball. My first thought is: he can't be the Pimpernel, then. My second is: where is this Pimpernel now we need him? And my third is: why can't I be seven feet tall? But I'm not, nor is the Geek. It looks like it's going to be the screaming charge, then.

I take a deep breath, give a nod to the Geek, grip the handle...and then suddenly I'm shoved out of the way. And here's Blake piled high with white boxes, shoeboxes. 'Sorry, Trokka,' he says in a silly singsong, his chin resting on the top box. 'Make way for Father Christmas.'

Christmas isn't for another three months.

And then he's past me and inside the classroom, and I, like a dummy, am still at the door, watching him hand out presents to all the Bins – runners of course, Blake's runners. Jaco's not so pleased but his gang ignore him. They're jostling round Blake, slapping him on the back, pulling out the shoes, kicking off their old ones, perching on the desks and Blake is in the middle smiling his dim smile and nodding away as Stef goes on about the last pair of trainers he bought. Stef is not only a bully and stupid, he is seriously boring, so boring I wonder how Jaco can put up with him.

Talk about lucky timing, I think. I look at the Geek. She shrugs. We go in. Crocker, forgotten now, makes his way round the group of excited Bins. He glances once at Blake, then he sits down at his desk and stares straight ahead. I don't ask him if he's all right because I reckon that will only make him feel worse.

The Bins are hyper, bouncing up and down in their new trainers, bashing into each other in a mad mosh. 'Wicked!' They're going. 'Weeck...eddd!

Right! All right!' Meanwhile Father Christmas Blake gathers the packaging and takes it out of the classroom.

A moment later a first former pokes his head round the door and tells Stef that he's wanted by Sir Pent. Stef saunters out, like he's trying not to bounce up on his toes in his new runners.

I check my spy mirror is still in place, and five minutes later the bell goes and the class streams back in. When Dorner comes in, he spots Stef's empty desk but when he's told where he is, he just carries on.

The odd thing, though, is that the desk remains empty for the rest of the morning. I notice that Jaco, who wasn't at all bothered to begin with, now keeps glancing at it and then at the door. The rest of us make a point of not noticing. Perhaps he fell down the toilet and drowned himself. Dream on.

At lunch there's an announcement from Sir Pent. The winners of the competition have all been decided and 'Three of the cleverest pupils in the country come from this school!' There's polite clapping from the seniors, and excited cheering from the younger pupils who haven't been here long enough to know better. I see Charlie Crocker look excited for a split second and then the mask comes down again. So he's gone in for this competition – why wouldn't he? After one week here who wouldn't want to win a place on a year-long cruise. Only those who know better than to trust Sir Pent, that's who.

'...names of the lucky winners will be revealed on national news tonight and,' says Sir Pent, winding his words round himself like a white silk scarf, 'there will be a little feature on the school.' More polite clapping. No cheering from the juniors though; they don't know what he's talking about. What he means, of course, is that there will be an interview with him. Next stop, Prime Minister.

'Jaco sounded cross with Blake,' mutters the Geek. We are at one end of the table and she's beside me.

'I saw you standing behind them. Do you know why he was cross?'

'Jealous. Didn't like his gang getting those shoes. Blake told him not to worry, theirs weren't quite top of the range.' She concentrates on her food, picking out the vegetables and nibbling the less soggy bits of green. 'He's really stuck in with them, isn't he? Didn't think he'd be that sort.'

'Maybe that's how you get to be rich.'

I look across to where he's sitting, down the far end of the table in among a whole bunch of Bins, Jaco included, so he can't have been that cheesed off.

The first formers at the table behind us finish their lunch and leave in a crowd, all bunched together, pushing and shoving, like they always do. One of them stumbles up against me and the Geek and then the duty master has a go at them and they're gone through the door.

A moment later I put my hand in my pocket and find a folded slip of paper. I carefully unfold it; another message, one word: 'GYM'. It's the same spiky writing as on my desk.

I slide it over to the Geek. 'Special delivery,' she says. 'Neat.'

The Bins beside Blake stand up and come towards us. Very casually the Geek crumples the scrap of paper and drops it into the stewy mess on her plate, and then stirs it in with her fork. 'You don't think it's a trap, do you?'

'For us? Who'd want to trap us?'

'Jaco.'

'You think he's taken up drawing flowers?'

She shrugs. 'They want to catch him, don't they? And that first thing they set up didn't work, did it?'

'I don't think he's that cunning.'

'You mean, you *hope* he's not that cunning.'

'Yeah.' I agree. 'I hope he's not.'

Chapter 14

The gym is directly above the kitchens but to get to it, we have to go down the long classroom corridor, through the changing rooms, with their damp concrete and peeling green paint, me through the boys, the Geek through the girls, and then out through a boot room and down the steps to the asphalt yard. Across that are the service doors to the kitchen and a couple of industrial-sized plastic waste bins. The other side of these is a flight of iron steps that lead directly up and into the gym – a shadowy hall dangled with ropes and odd things designed to cause pain. It's not a place I go to through choice. Two months ago, at the end of the summer term, Jaco held a competition for himself and the Bins – 'just for a lark' – to see how many swots they could hang upside down from the top bars. By the end of the afternoon there were forty kids all in a row, like dead birds, except a few of them were crying and dead birds don't cry. I got wind of what they were up to so I hid under the wooden horse – I saw and heard everything.

'What do you think?'

The asphalt yard is deserted. No one lingers here. It is just an enclosed space you cross to get to the gym, or to the back of the kitchens. It makes me think of prison, of ambushes.

The Geek shrugs. 'Go to the gym, of course.'

'And if we're caught?'

'Are you scared, Patroclus?'

Surrounded by Bins, being picked on, dumped into muck, getting hurt...yes, of course I'm frightened. 'All the time,' I say and hurry down the steps, The Geek following. We start walking smartly across the asphalt – no point running – better to look as if you're carrying out a job for someone.

I can hear the muffled banging and clatter of pots and dishes from the kitchen and voices shouting. One of the voices doesn't sound as if it's coming from the kitchen at all.

The Geek slows.

'Keep going,' I tell her.

'Can't you hear it? Someone's stuck in one of

those big container things.'

She means the kitchen waste skips. They're not the sort of containers you can accidentally fall into. They're chest-high, with swing lids, so you can tip in the slop easily. When a skip's full, kitchen helpers flip a bar down that locks the lid.

'Patroclus, stop!'

I stop but all my usual warning voices are saying: 'Don't check it out! It's someone else's problem!' If Jaco or his mates spot us we'll end up buried alive... But that was the old me. The before-this-term me. The before-the-Pimpernel me.

'OK.' We hurry towards the skips. I can hear the calling more clearly now but it's mangled, like someone gargling with their mouth full of food.

'It's the one on the right,' I say. The one that's already been locked.

The bar slides up easily and I flip up the lid. The first things I see are a smeary pair of very familiar-looking runners. The only people to wear those are Jaco and the Bins, and Percy Blake. I look at the Geek.

'Is it him?' she says.

'Orfmer-atta-eer' skurgles the head squished down in yesterday's cabbage.

'Soon find out.' I hoick myself up onto the rim of

the skip and, trying to hold my breath so as not to gag on the sloppy food stink, I grab the legs in both my arms.

Across the yard from us, a figure appears in the doorway to the changing rooms. It's too late to disappear, so I just grit my teeth and heave. The body comes up with a shuffle and rustle and then a gigantic splutter. And what a prize!

'Who is it?'

I don't know whether to cheer or sneer or simply leg it out of there as, with a groan, a very grubby Stef slowly sits up and grips the edge of the skip, ready to lever himself up and out. I break the news to the Geek.

She pulls a face. 'Him! You shouldn't have bothered.' Now she tells me!

'Did you trip, then?' I ask Stef, who's busy trying to wipe the muck from his mouth with the filthy end of his T-shirt.

'Nah, watcha think I am, some sort of git?'

I have my polite 'no comment' face on.

'Someone done it to me. Big bloke, must have been.' He screws up his rat face and thinks for a moment – difficult operation, that, for Stef, normally Jaco does all his thinking for him. 'Or a gang, maybe,' He sticks a dirty finger in his mouth and pulls out some stringy green stuff.

It's time to move. I look back to the changing rooms. The figure hasn't moved but I can't make out the face as it's in shadow. The Geek, seeing me look, glances over her shoulder. 'Come on, get down, Patroclus.'

'You all right then, Stef?' Nothing like thanking us; that would be a thought too many for Stef. I swing myself over the side and drop down.

'Oi, wait!' Stef's ratty face is closed up with suspicion. 'I got a message to go to the gym an' all, from Jaco, and then I got jumped. Don't know anything about it I suppose?'

'Me? I never know anything, Stef, you know that.'

'Who's that with you?' he peers down at us, stringy bits of muck hanging from his ears. 'Oh, the weird-looking one. Yabba, innit. Yabbajabba.'

He's not strong on charm.

'Mention this to anyone and you're dead, right?'

'No!' The Geek snaps, her eyes giant black cannonballs behind her thick lenses.

'Wha'?'

'You cause us any trouble at all, or to that Charlie Crocker, and the whole school, every single first-year, is going to know exactly where we found you. Get it?'

Stef's mouth drops down like the back of a dumper truck. I grab the Geek's arm and pull her away before she jumps up and bites him or he has a heart attack – either way we would get the blame.

'Forget about him. What about the gym? Have we got time?'

'We weren't meant to go to the gym; we were meant to find him.' The bell for lessons goes and she pulls her arm free and starts walking quickly back towards the changing rooms.

'But the note said the gym!'

I glance back at Stef, who is standing up on the top of the skip like a marooned rubbishy Robinson Crusoe. ''Ere,' he yells, 'wait for me!'

We ignore him.

'Don't tell me you didn't see it, Patroclus.'

'What?'

'On the gym-side of the skip, the sign, the red flower. He wanted us to find Stef.'

'He? The Pimpernel? Why would he want to do that?'

'Don't know, but I reckon we'll find out pretty soon.'

'You saw that person watching us?'

'Yes.'

'You think it was him?'

'Maybe.' She pushes the door open, and there sitting on the bench facing us is Percy Blake, trying on a pair of blood-red Blake runners.

Chapter 15

'You!'

'Me? What do you mean, me?' Blake acts as if he's surprised. Well maybe he is but not more than me; what's he doing, sitting where he shouldn't be sitting, taking off one pair of expensive runners and putting on another, brand new but a different colour.

'Was there someone who just went through here?'

'No idea, Trokka. Only popped in to change; the morning pair got a bit grubby.' He gives his silly laugh. 'Maroon,' he says, holding up the new pair to show us. 'What do you think?'

The Geek ignores his silly question. 'Were you spying on us?'

Blake's expression is hard to judge under those

fake glasses of his. Funny the way they make him look so dim while the Geek in her mega-specs can look fierce as anything. It's as if they come from different planets, which in a way I suppose they do. He shrugs and then bends down to finish tucking his laces in behind the foamy tongue of his runners. He admires the result, twisting his feet one way and then the other, flicks off an imaginary speck of dust and then stands up. I feel like giving him a good shake but I don't think it would make any difference. 'Saw you rescue poor what's-his-name; the ugly one with the teeth. Jaco'll be pleased with you. Shall I tell him?'

'No.'

'Classrooms!' roars the duty master and then a moment later we can hear a banging sound moving down the corridor. The usual after-lunch routine: all the doors get banged, anyone then late back into class is put in next Saturday's Swotshop, no arguing.

'Better dash,' says Blake. I don't know why, he's never bothered about being late before and he seems to be the one exception to Staleways' rules and regulations - because of his dad of course. 'Keep up the good work! ' and he's out of the door.

'Did you think it was going to be Blake?'

She pulls a face. 'Him? No, I didn't.'

'What did he mean by "the good work"?'

'Nothing. It's just the way he talks, posh like his old man. But it's still a funny coincidence, isn't it, him being the one in here?'

'Yeah...' I'm thinking and feeling an idea coming on '...but this Pimpernel could still be anyone. He's the x, like in a problem, c+m=x.' She looks blank. 'Clues plus motive equals the Pimpernel.'

'Patroclus, thinking in maths isn't any good to us. Anyone who's not a Bin would give their eye-teeth to dump Stef in kitchen muck. I tell you, the only real clue we've got is the one he leaves behind him.'

I pull a face; I thought the formula was neat.

'And what's it matter? He knows us, leaves us messages. He's on our side.'

'If he's on our side, why doesn't he make himself known?'

'He's got to be sure of us, that's why. Stop fussing.' There's a loud voice in the corridor. 'Let's go back quick before we get into more trouble.'

The Geek ducks through to the girls' changing room while I follow the way Blake went. I get to my seat about twenty seconds before the Geek scurries into the classroom, just as the late-bell sounds. 'The skin of your teeth, Yabba,' sneers Jaco. 'Where did you spend your lunch hour?'

'Keeping out of trouble,' says the Geek, ducking her head, and to my astonishment she begins to cry quietly and doesn't stop even when Mr Dorner comes in and begins the lesson.

Jaco nods as if he knows something, and smiles. Unhappy pupils make him feel good. The Geek, she's so smart. I hadn't realised that she could act. Wake up, Patroclus, I tell myself, she's going to walk away with the Oscars if you're not careful.

We've science in the afternoon and though the Geek looks like a brainbox, her acting skills don't help her with the test. She and Blake get equal last in the class. I'm quite good at science; at least, I like designing things, lifts and pulleys and stuff like that. I reckon I could have built the pyramids no problem and without a thousand slaves too. I don't come top though, no way. I always answer the last five questions on a scrap of paper and then slip it in my pocket and check the answers later. Crocker gets top; he looks worried but defiant; like he doesn't care any more. I reckon he's pinning his hopes on the competition.

Stef pitches up when we've finished. He stands at the door but refuses to come in or explain himself when Dorner asks him where he's been. 'None of yer business,' he growls sulkily. 'I wanna speak to Jaco.'

Mr Dorner ignores the rudeness. He has to, probably written into his contract. Jaco leans back in his chair. 'What do you want, Stef?'

'A word. Something happened, dinnit?'

Jaco gets up, all theatrical, knowing everyone's watching but pretending not to. I am hoping that Stef won't say anything about us rescuing him. Jaco's not thick; he'll want to know what me and the Geek were doing out there together.

When he comes back in, Jaco's not looking so pleased any more. But he doesn't look at me or the Geek so I imagine Stef told it his way: mugged by giant thugs or something. 'Bin meeting!' Jaco announces curtly from the door. Maggot and the two other Bins in the class, the Sullen Brothers, get up and without so much as an 'excuse me' to Dorner, they walk out.

They don't come back that afternoon but I'm nervous about after school; they'll be planning something and it's going to be tricky to escape without getting duffed up at the very least.

It's only when we're packing up after the last bell and I'm checking through my books, selecting which ones to take home, that I see another message.

Automatically I twist around to see if anyone is looking at me. No one. This is the fourth one of the day if I include the scribbled pimpernel flower on the kitchen waste bin; and that's not counting the ones Sir Pent found. He's been busy, our Pimpernel. This message is in the tiniest writing, this time on the inside of a scrumpled-up KitKat wrapper. I don't eat KitKats so I checked it; I also don't leave scrumpled-up bits of paper in my desk. I'm tidy – can't help it. This is what the message says: 'You did well.' What's that mean? In my test? By rescuing Stef from green slime? And then underneath: 'Expect to hear from me tonight.' That's it, apart from the squiggled flower.

I tear up the wrapper into little bits and scatter it into the bin by the door. I wonder if the Geek got one too but she's already left. And I wonder how this mysterious Pimpernel is going to get in touch next time; pigeon maybe, he seems to like complicated things. I head for the exit and Bin Alley, where the Bins make a double line that leads all the way from the front door to the gate and we, all the swots, have to go down the middle. Great. Officially, it's meant to make the end of school neat and tidy, give a good impression to the parents. Really it's just a good opportunity for them to have a go at us, mainly the younger ones, of course.

Sure enough, when I'm coming down the steps I can see they're shouting at the young ones, giving them a shake, emptying some of their bags. There's not much purpose to it. They obviously don't know anything, just giving a show of strength. No teachers around, of course. Sometimes I wonder who really runs the school.

I see Blake up ahead of me, the Geek a couple of paces away from him. Then just as we get near the beginning of the alley, Blake seems to be right beside the Geek and the two of them walk through with no problem. I get hauled out, though. 'What do you know, Trokka?' says Jaco. 'An oilbag like you always knows something.'

'Know about what?' I'm all innocence of course.

Jaco jabs me with his forefinger. 'Just about everything, Trokka.' He jabs me again, really hard, and I try not to wince. 'Collapsing desks, yeah? Grease on the floor, yeah? Stef getting mugged, yeah? Got anything to do with this Mr Pimpy the tag artist, has it?'

So, I wasn't far wrong. Him getting tipped in a bin has turned into a mugging.

'Yes,' which is what I guess the Pimpernel wants me to say. Why else leave little tags like he does?

'And what's so special about him, yeah?'

I shrug. 'Like a hero. Secret. What do you want me to say?'

'You're off your trolley, Trokka,' he sneers. 'Too much olive oil. Get out of here.'

I grab my bag and do a head-down scuttle. When I reach the gate I glance back and Jaco is standing back from the line of Bins, looking my way. What does he suspect?

Back home, I do my work, or try to. Two hours till the news comes on and we get to hear who the winners are. At five to six the doorbell rings. Could this be him? Not pigeons but in person! I clatter down the stairs and fling open the door.

It's the Geek. 'I got a message,' she says.

'From him? The Pimpernel? Telling you to come here?'

She grins. 'You look funny.'

I don't think I do at all but I let her in.

Chapter 16

Exactly five minutes later the telephone rings. My mother answers and because she always picks up the phone in the café where there's noisy chatter in the background she can never hear properly. 'It's a Mr Pindlnindeyl,' she shouts, 'for you, Michael. You take it upstairs. I put him down here.'

I turn down the TV and pick up the receiver. 'Hello,' I say. 'Who is this?'

'You know who I am,' says the voice and I'm sure I should recognise it but I can't say I can – maybe it's the phone, makes everyone sound a bit fuzzy. 'Is Minou with you?'

'Yes.'

'Turn on your computer.'

How does he know I have one?

'Is it on?'

'Yes.'

'Log on to the chatline.' Then the phone clicks. I log on and the little icon flicks up to say I have a message. I open it.

'What is it?' whispers the Geek, who's followed me upstairs.

'Him.'

The Geek leans over my shoulder to read the screen with me: 'Do you want to join me?'

I look at the Geek. She nods.

I type 'yes' and then: 'Who are you really?' and press reply.

Half a second later. 'You know.'

'The Pimpernel's made up, not real.' I type.

'I am real,' comes the reply.

'How can we trust you?'

'You already trust me.'

I look at the Geek. 'Do we?' I mouth at her, as if he could hear. She nods.

Another line blinks up on the screen. 'Can I trust you? Can I trust you? Can I trust you...' the question keeps repeating until the screen is almost full. Then there's a pause but before I can answer, there's another question. 'Is your TV on?' Weird.

'Go on,' says the Geek. 'What are you waiting for?'

I type 'yes'.

'Watch the news.' And then the message icon clicks off. We both turn back to the telly.

The Geek turns up the sound and there is Sir Pent, with his 'sincere' look swelling across the whole screen. The voice over tells us that Staleways is a model school, a flagship with the most incredible exam results – this is news to me; I knew they were good but not that good. It makes me wonder what the rest of the country's schools are like.

'Michael, are you watching this thing?' shouts my mother from the foot of the stairs.

'Yes, mum.'

'Why did you not win! I do not understand you.'

'Yes mum.'

The winners line up on the stage in the school, mostly fresh keen-looking pupils with big happy faces and a few that we recognise – Charlie Crocker is one. And Tim Tarker and Ben Porliss, grinning like monkeys. Between them they've clocked up enough hours in the Swotshop to deserve a luxury trip to the moon. It won't happen though. There is loads of hand-shaking of course and the winners then trail out to where three black-windowed stretch limos are waiting to take them straight to their cruise ship down in Southampton.

'Stretch limos,' sighs the Geek. Funny, I didn't think that would impress her.

'Typical Sir Pent,' I say sourly and switch off the set.

The computer makes its 'I'm alive again' sound and there's the Pimpernel.

'Is it for real?' he writes.

Without even consulting the Geek, I tap 'no'.

'Will something happen to the winners?'

'Yes.'

'Explain.'

'One, because it's Sir Pent who dreamed this up and he doesn't do anything for charity. Two, because if it was really going to be a good prize you can bet anything that Jaco or one of the other Bins would somehow have been wangled in there as a winner.'

Pause. Then he types: 'You've missed three.'

'What's three?'

'The boat they're meant to be going on doesn't exist.'

'That can't be true,' says the Geek.

I type: 'How do you know that?'

'Checked the shipping register.'

I didn't even know there was something called a

shipping register. I'm impressed. 'What does it mean then?'

The screen flickers emptily for a moment. Then: 'Don't know.' Pause. Then, once again: 'Can I trust you?'

Does he know what Jaco asked me? Does he know that for one fleeting moment, as I was drifting off to sleep, I did have that thought, telling Jaco what I had found out; but I'd never do it, not in a million years. All the same, I feel my ears redden. 'YES!' I type.

Then: 'I'll make contact soon.' And that's it. Not much of a one for hellos and goodbyes. Very businesslike.

The Geek and I look at each other.

'Supposing they're in real danger,' she says. 'Supposing he plans to kill them...supposing he's going to...'

'He's not going to kill anyone because that won't get him any profit,' I say, interrupting her.

'But he's going to do something, isn't he?'

'Yes, but we have to wait.'

And this is only the end of day one.

The next morning, splashed across the newspapers

and blasting out of the radio: Cruise liner disappears without trace only hours after leaving harbour. Twenty talented students and an entire ship's crew missing.

My mother weeps and hugs me. My father weeps and hugs me. My family is big on crying. My sister doesn't weep but then she would have quite liked me to have been on the boat. 'You stay at home, Michael. There will be no school today. You will see,' my mother says.

Not go to school? On any other day of the year maybe, not today though. Something stinks worse than Stef with a face full of old cabbage, and I want to find out what it is; and I don't have to phone the Geek to know she'll think the same.

Who was the idiot who thought that at least nothing serious would happen to the prizewinners? Me.

I don't think they're dead though. Wouldn't make sense. That's what I keep telling myself.

Chapter 17

Numb. Totally numb. I stumble going up to my bedroom and bang my arm against the wall. I don't feel a thing. I turn on the computer and log on. Nothing. No message from the Pimpernel. I don't know what I expected, but something, maybe a miracle to say it wasn't true. I want to talk to the Geek but I'll be seeing her in ten minutes so what's the point in picking up the phone. I pack my things and head for school.

Faces longer than the Blackwall tunnel and twice as gloomy? Of course, Sir Pent knows how to do misery for the TV cameras. It's fake of course, more fake than my sister's stick-on eyelashes. The Bins are still the same though, strutting around like football champions, while Mr Robestone has a flinty glint in his eye, snapping off barbed one-liners that could sting a saint.

It's only us, the swots, the mice, who are really affected by the news. Everybody shuffles between lessons, not talking because they don't know what to say. I'm the same, though I'm keeping my eyes peeled; Pent's got some nasty business going. I'm sure of it.

We even avoid looking at Charlie's desk, all of us apart from Jaco and his pals of course. Maggot claims that the world's better off without swots 'cause they just get up your nose; Maggot has a big face and an ugly little nose. Jaco props a note up on the empty seat that says: 'TO RENT' which gives the Bins a laugh – about the only time I have seen the Sullen Brothers smile, typical isn't it? I want to scrumple up the note and ram it down Jaco's throat, but I don't and I feel so small I wish I would disappear completely.

Then, out of the blue, there's an explosion from ice-cool Sally. She stomps up to the desk, snatches up the note and, right in front of Jaco, tears it into little pieces and throws the bits at him and then goes back to her place. Jaco doesn't say anything, just smirks and nods at the others.

The odd thing is that there is another empty space: Blake's not in today – probably off with his dad somewhere grand. Nor is there a message from the Pimpernel in my desk – nothing first thing this morning and nothing now. Was it all talk and small stuff? If Sally is cross enough to make a protest, surely we should be doing something? Squiggling little red flowers and being a secret gang is nothing unless we tip Staleways upside down and shake Sir Pent out of his lair.

He's responsible. He's guilty from his horrible head down to his crêpe-soled shoes. And it hits me, smack, like I've been whacked by one of my dad's frying pans. He's guilty as sin and, if the Pimpernel's not around, me and the Geek have to show the world what Sir Pent's really like. This is it – we're in the spotlight now.

I am not numb anymore. I'm angry. I can feel anger burning me up right from the tips of my toes to the skin on my scalp. I am sure they all know something. The Geek and I snatch a quick hushed word at break.

'Calm down, Trokka.'

'I am calm!'

'You're waving your arms around and there are two Bins watching us.'

I stick my hands in my pockets. 'We need to do something and I don't think we should wait for him...'

'Not so loud.'

'...all right, but for him to tell us.'

'He has.'

'What?'

She shows me a blank CD. 'Found it on my doorstep this morning. Here.' She snakes an earphone lead out of her inner pocket and passes it to me. 'Listen.'

There's a snatch of music and then a voice that I don't quite recognise is speaking: 'Search high, do you understand me, and search low. Something very important is being hidden from us. Remember there's no smoke without fire. Are you listening, Patroclus? No smoke without fire.' And then the music swept in again. Well, not pigeon post but still pretty complicated. I mean recording a CD, couldn't he just phone?

'Oi! No headphones. Give it me, Trokka.' It's Stef, on his own too. Funny, having seen him upside down, he doesn't worry me at all. But I act quickly.

I push the Geek away from me and snap: 'Shove off!' She doesn't even hesitate, just turns on her heel and runs off down the corridor, round the corner and out of sight.

I turn back to Stef. 'Give you what, Stef?'

He's looking confused; pupils don't question the Bins.

I hold out my hands. 'I've got nothing, Stef. Not a thing.'

'Her, then.'

'Don't know who you're talking about.'

And before he can think of an answer to this flat lie, I have skirted round him and nipped down past the junior classrooms. I check that he's not following me, then I go out to the front, where I catch up with the Geek again, over by the iron railings – our meeting place.

'Did you understand the message?' she asks. 'What does it mean, 'search high, and search low'?'

'The Pimpernel must want us to break into the Serpent's office.'

'And low?'

'Basement. Where the Swotshop is.' I'm fired up. This is it – I mean I've even got an idea buzzing, but then it's like the brakes come on a bit, you know. 'But what exactly are we looking for? I mean is it stuff to do with the competition?'

'Of course.' She always seems so sure of herself. 'And maybe there's more, Patroclus, maybe he's into all sorts of criminal schemes. You know: secret funds. Embezzlement.' She nods like she's waiting for me to ask what it means.

I am not going to be impressed. 'Nicking money, you mean, but in a sneaky way? Am I right?'

'Yes.'

'OK, so are you on for it? Could be dangerous.'

'Of course,' and she starts to talk about waiting for the weekend and the school being empty so I interrupt her.

'We don't have to wait. We can do it during fire practice.'

'When's that?'

I grin. 'When I set off the alarm.'

No time like the present. No one in my family says that. We are a strictly tomorrow family. Sure, my father always says, no problem, tomorrow is good. But his life doesn't run to bells and five-minute warnings; ours does.

'Good thinking, Patroclus. Maybe that's what he meant about smoke and fire.'

I thought it had been my idea, not his.

'How do we set it off?'

'The kitchens.'

We slip past the football players, and nip round the edge of the building into the yard where we had found Stef head-down yesterday. And then we run quickly over to the kitchen door. I've only ever peered into the kitchens from the dining room but I know there's an office just by this outer door and there are going to be smoke sensors everywhere; it's the law, I know, because we have to have them in our own kitchen.

Carefully, I try the door. Unlocked. I'd hoped it would be, but it means that some of the kitchen staff will be in there. How to get them out, that's the problem.

'When I tell you,' I say to the Geek, 'I want you to bang on the door and when someone comes to open it, you have to say Mr Robestone told you to tell them that their waste bin's been knocked over and it needs to be dealt with immediately.'

'OK, but it hasn't.'

I ignore this. 'As soon as you've told them, leg it for the changing rooms and then when you hear the alarm, head for the Serpent's stairway. When you see him coming down, you go and check his office. Look for anything connected with the competition, anything at all. I'll take the basement. We'll have about ten minutes while the whole school goes out into the front yard; that's all. Are you ready?'

'Of course, but I'm not running anywhere. I told you that before.'

'That's up to you; just don't get caught. OK?' She

154

nods and then I grip the top of the bin and by hanging on the lip and leaning right back I manage to get it off balance and then it's an easy matter to send it over with a crash, letting a mound of cans and sloppy goo come spilling out.

I nip over to stand beside the door and the Geek then gives a sharp rap, once, twice and then the door is shoved open, hiding me completely.

The Geek does her routine. The catering manager, a gigantic man with shirtsleeves rolled up and a blue dragon winding round his thick forearm, can already see the mess. He curses and calls back over his shoulder for Mickey to come and give him a hand. Then a moment later, they are righting the bin and shovelling muck back into it. The Geek has walked smartly off, in case they remember to ask for her name, while I slip, quick as a rat, round the door and into the kitchen.

My dad would throw a fit if he saw a kitchen like this one. It's out of the dark ages and it doesn't look as if it has been cleaned since then either. Dirty sinks to the right, dirty work surfaces to the left. The cookers, crusted with black, run down the middle of the room where two giant black pots simmer and gurgle. The air is thick with steam and the smell of boiling greens. Sinks to the right, office to the left, a jungle of spikes with bits of paper jabbed onto them. What I want is the smoke detector. There has to be one. Yes! Over by the door leading to the hall.

Matches?

I hadn't thought about that. In the office. Please. Please. It stinks of stale cigarettes. And there's a lighter. I grab it and run down the narrow aisle, holding my breath as I pass the bubbling pots. I flick the lighter, it catches first time and I hold it up. Nothing. Come on. I try again, jumping to get closer to the sensor. There is very little advantage to being small like me. Right now it's a curse. I glance back to the door. Any second, they're going to be coming back.

Nothing for it. Back to the office, grab the chair, back down the aisle. Flip the lighter and ram it as close to the sensor as I can. 1, 2, 3...

The ear-splitting jangle of the alarm going off nearly makes me fall off the chair. Will they come back or go to the assembly point round the front of the school?

The far door swings open as I'm dropping to my knees and backing away round the end cooker, dragging the chair with me. If I can't get the lighter and chair back into the office, someone is going to put two and two together.

'Turn off the veg, Mickey, and check nothing else is on. Then get out to the front. Move it!'

That's it. I stick the lighter in my pocket and duck backwards into the hall, pulling the chair with me. Fingers crossed there's no one here. No, good. I leave the chair. At least it won't be an immediate giveaway. How long have we got? I glance at my watch. Ten minutes? I can't remember how long the drills take, not that long, but this time, they'll have to call the fire brigade to check the building. Could be longer. No time to waste though.

Thin strips of reddish light slant down from the high windows into the gloomy hall. I crawl on hands and knees across to the door we use, check the coast is clear and then slip out into the entrance lobby where the stairs are.

The lobby and corridor are still jammed with pupils and shouting red-faced teachers. I worm my way to the back of the crowd so I'm right by the stairs that go down to the Swotshop. Then with a quick glance to check no one is looking my way, I take one, then a second step down the stairs. This is it. I turn and scuttle down as quick as I can, down into the dark, or what should be dark.

No one is going to be down here, surely. The Swotshop is only used for detention at the weekends. But strangely there is a single light on in the corridor. No sign of anyone though. I check the Swotshop door. Locked. I peer through the keyhole. Dark. OK, no point in wasting time. I run down the corridor, checking doors, none open – store rooms, I presume, or boiler and pipes and things like that. It is warm down here, warm and dampish. The corridor comes to a stop with a dead end. I try the other way. I pass the light and then about ten steps later, I come to another flight of stairs, going down. And there is a big red sign telling me that this is strictly out of bounds. Why? Is there something hidden down here?

Three minutes since I set off the alarm. I have maybe got the same amount of time before I need to get out and join the school.

I take a breath and head down, wondering how many levels there are under Staleways. My rubber soles slap softly against the concrete steps, but my breath sounds loud in my ears.

I reach the bottom step and without pausing to check I swing right. Another long corridor, with a single orange light casting a dim glow ahead of me. Doors to the left and right, one of them metal and a 2 painted on it. Level 2? Swotshop 2? Why would Pent have another Swotshop? It's locked. No point trying the others then and no time. Time to head back.

Two seconds later I'm halfway down the corridor, when I come skidding to a halt and my heart thunks in my chest. There's the Serpent! His back to me. Where did he come from? And what's he doing down here? No time to hang around and ask questions. Too late.

'Hey! Come back! I know who you are! You come back here, this minute!'

No, sir, not me, because it's not the time to forget the rules: run away if you can! And boy, can I run fast when I have to!

He's running too and shouting. His voice is echoing around me but I have the edge. Up, up I go. Along the top corridor, past the Swotshop. Final flight of stairs. Pause. Breathe. Check the front hall. No one. I run down past the classrooms and nip out through the changing rooms. Yes, I've done it, given him the slip. Not bad, Patroclus. I check my watch: six minutes. Our time is almost up.

Chapter 18

Keeping my fingers crossed that the roll call isn't finished yet, and that the Geek is safely back, I sneak round the outside of the changing rooms and join the tail end of the school that's still milling around by the front gate.

Where is she? I look everywhere and start shoving my way through the crowd but there's no sign of her anywhere and then I suddenly feel a hand gripping my collar.

'Patroclus, why aren't you standing with your class? Your name's already been called twice.' Mr Dorner ticks his clipboard while I mumble excuses which he doesn't bother to listen to.

Where is the Geek? All she had to do was take a quick look in the Serpent's study if the coast was clear. Behind Dorner I can see Sir Pent standing on the school's front steps, scanning the crowd. He looks unruffled, as always when he's in public; but he didn't sound calm about three minutes ago when he was yelling after me; he sounded like he wanted to mash me into little pieces. I see him having a word with Mr Robestone, who shakes his head. Then he consults with the other teachers, one by one. Did he get a good look? I bet I know what he's asking. Keep your head down, Patroclus, and think very small.

He comes down to where Dorner is standing. 'Anyone missing, Mr Dorner?'

Dorner glances at his clipboard. 'Yes,' he says after half a moment, 'Minou Yabba. I haven't seen her yet, Headmaster.'

Sir Pent nods. 'Minou Yabba,' he repeats, his eye wandering over our class, but I get the feeling he's trying to fix what she looks like and match it to the figure he glimpsed running away from him, rather than thinking about us.

At that moment there is a hustle of excitement as the fire engine pulls up and the firemen come running through and into the main building.

'As soon as you find her, I want her sent to me, directly.' Sir Pent gives Dorner a curt nod and walks smartly back up to the entrance to speak to the chief fireman.

My palms are sweating.

She's going to get caught, I just know it. And if she's up in the Pent House when they find her, it won't just be Saturday morning in the Swotshop. He'll slice her into bits.

I keep looking around. I can't help it. The Pimpernel's got to be here somewhere. And I need him now – not one of his messages – but him. I don't know what to do.

Over to the right, Jaco and a squad of Bins are moving through the school, checking names, herding and pushing swots into lines. Our class gets shoved towards the front.

Then there's a flurry of activity round the doorway and everyone around me is craning forward to see and people are asking what's going on. I see a stocky fireman barging through the main door and he's got someone held in his arms.

'Who is it?' and someone else says: 'Who is she?'

It has to be the Geek! And she's unconscious or dead or...

Without thinking, I start to move forward. Someone grabs my arm: 'What you think you're doing, Trokka?' It's Jaco but I tug myself free and maybe there's something about the look I give him because for the first time he doesn't say anything else, just gives a shrug and turns away.

And then I'm at the foot of the steps and the Serpent and his cronies are clustering round the fireman who carried out the Geek and who, with the fire chief and another officer, is now laying her down on the ground.

'No sign of fire, sir,' says the chief officer, 'not in the entire building. But it looks like the sensor went off in the kitchen. No obvious cause so I'm afraid it might have been set off deliberate...'

'Did you see anything? A message, perhaps, a note? No?'

'Why on earth would there be a note?' says the fire officer. He sounds cross.

Sir Pent points down at the Geek. 'What about her? Where was she?' he says coldly. 'Was she in the kitchen?'

'No, sir,' says the stocky fireman.

I swear that Sir Pent shudders slightly, a ripple that ends with a long sniff. 'I see. It doesn't matter. We'll deal with her now.'

'She needs medical attention.'

'Nonsense! She's in trouble; a halfwit could tell that she's faking.'

The fireman ignores the insult. 'I don't think so,'

he says.

'And I *do* think so,' says Sir Pent, 'and grateful as I am,' he sounds about as grateful as I do when Jaco has nicked all my chocolate, 'I would suggest this is school business, and nothing to do with you. Now, can the school go back in and resume lessons?'

The fire chief nods and Robestone, who has been standing stiff as a spike through this whole exchange, jerks into action, and instantly teachers and Bins are barking commands and the school begins to file past the little group still standing around the Geek, and back into the building.

I manage to hang back, standing behind the firemen so that the Serpent can't see me but to anyone else it looks like I'm in some way part of the group.

'Where did you find her? Down in the basement? Strictly out of bounds, if that's where she was.'

'No. In the toilets...'

'Oh, hiding, no doubt because I know she was downstairs, running away from me when I caught her.' So he does think it was her, not me.

'You caught her, did you? Was it you then who authorised her to be stuffed head-first into the waste bin in the girls' toilets?' The question is delivered cool as a peeled peach. 'Couldn't breathe.

That's why I'd say she lost consciousness.'

The Bins got her! Is that why Jaco backed off? Knows he'd gone too far this time? 'Oh,' says Sir Pent. 'Ah. Yes.' He swivels towards Robestone. 'Do you know anything of this?' It is the first time he has even acknowledged his deputy is standing beside him.

'No, Headmaster.'

'Could be a case for the police,' suggests the fireman. 'Dangerous assault.'

The Geek stirs.

Sir Pent undergoes one of his transformations. 'Not at all,' he says smoothly. 'Thank you so much for your help, gentlemen. No doubt a prank. Now, Minou, are you all right?'

The Geek, with some difficulty, sits up and slowly rubs her forehead. 'Yes, I think so.'

Time to make a move. 'I'll take her back to the classroom, shall I, Sir?' I say, slipping in between the firemen and giving the Geek a hand to get up.

'Yes, of course. Just the thing, Patroclus,' and he actually smiles at me, relieved, I reckon, to have the problem disappear, which is just what I figured. 'Take your time, Yabba, no hurry, eh? Glass of water from the kitchen, perhaps.'

As we walk away, I whisper: 'Are you OK?'

'Of course.'

'Did you get binned by Jaco?'

'Nah.' She chuckles. 'Got in myself – getting in wasn't so hard, but I'm glad there wasn't a real fire. Getting out would have been a pig.'

'Lucky that fireman found you, then.' I notice that she's holding something, her left hand is closed into a fist and she keeps glancing at it. 'What's that you've got?' We're in the corridor outside the classroom. No one around and there's just the murmur of voices from the other side of the row of closed doors.

She opens her hand and there in her palm is a little scrap of creased paper. She smoothes it out. There it is, the familiar spidery writing 'Good news!' just that and then the flower!

'What's that mean?' She closes her hand into a fist. 'Did you see him?'

'No.'

'How did you get it? Did you find it in the Pent House?'

'No, never got in there. Door was locked.' Like me she's staring at the note, frowning slightly. 'We'll have to come back,' she says. 'Could try a window maybe, after school.'

I blink. A window means climbing up the outside

of the building.

'I tried to find you,' she says, 'but I was too late. Just managed to get to the girls' toilets and stick myself in the bin as the firemen were coming in through the door. The note got pressed into my hand when they were pulling me out, but I didn't see who it was.'

'The Pimpernel a fireman! One of them! Which one?'

'You were the one who had his eyes open, Trokka. I fainted, remember?'

But what did I see? Firemen, and they all looked like...firemen; I didn't look at any faces.

Chapter 19

Empty desks. Blake's empty desk. The fireman. I'm all wired up; thoughts jumping this way and that like fleas on a cat. I try to picture the fireman who carried the Geek out. Was he the one who gave her the message? Was he the Pimpernel? If only I had looked at him properly. What an idiot. Was he a bit smaller than the others? I don't know, maybe. And the message: 'Good news'. What news? All I know is that it's a miracle me and the Geek are alive. If we'd been caught, Sir Pent would have sealed us up somewhere down on Level 2...or 3 – is there a 3 or a 4? How far down does it go? Or, I look at Charlie's empty desk, could it be...that the newspapers got it wrong? That would be more than good news. Do newspapers get it wrong? I don't know; doesn't seem likely.

Of course the lessons take an age to get going. I can't concentrate anyway: a history project about ancient Greece! 'Hades,' drones Mr Dorner, 'The underworld, mmm, a sort of hell I suppose...' Do you mind if I don't? My mum told me all the stories when I was little and my dad said 'Why you tell him old things? New is good. We like new now.' But all the songs he sings are old ones.

Anyway, I'm thinking this, and about the firemen and the Pimpernel and the crumpled bit of paper I've got in my pocket, when the Bins come back and the whole class suddenly wakes up. 'Held back for a meeting with Mr Robestone,' says Jaco. No apologies or nothing, just that. They all look angry too, like someone has had a go at them; they're not used to that.

'Very well,' says Mr Dorner, 'you can sit down then.'

But Jaco doesn't. He goes over to the Geek's desk and before she can say anything he slams open the lid, deliberately scattering the books she had on the top all over the place. 'Desk search,' he says bluntly, not even looking Dorner's way. 'Head's orders.' The Geek sits still, doesn't move a muscle; she's getting smart, picking up my rules without me even telling them to her. I bet she's raging though, eyes glaring behind those thick glasses – give a rat a heart attack just from looking. Jaco the rat better watch it.

'What are we looking for?' asks Mr Dorner.

'*You're* not looking for anything,' says Jaco rudely, 'we are,' and turns his back on Mr Dorner. You can hear the class taking a breath. Old Dorner himself looks like a stunned penguin. Then, rather slowly, he sits down at his desk and pretends to make notes in an exercise book. A moment later, he gives up, picks up a newspaper and disappears behind it.

We, at least all of us but the Geek, know the drill and stand up beside our desks, while Stef, the Maggot and Marco take a row each and go through all our belongings, nicking what they want while they're at it; that's if anyone's stupid enough to keep nickable stuff in their desk.

Stupid?

Stupid enough!

I suddenly remember what's in my desk: my spying mirrors, the little mirror stuck to the inside cover of my maths book. What are they going to make of that? And I've another one, a tiny scrap of mirror on a stick; I modelled it on the pokey mirrors our dentist uses for looking behind your teeth; I thought it would be handy for spying round corners. Handy! Handy for getting dragged off to the

Serpent!

'No chocca then, Trokka,' grunts Maggot, riffling through the first of my books with his stubby fingers.

And what if they go through our pockets? The Pimpernel note! That'll go down well – down a deep well all the way to Hades. Maybe if I can distract him, I think. 'Chocolate,' I say, 'is that what you're after?'

'Nah, don't be so thick, you Greek git. It's anything to do with the competition...' He has a way with words, does Maggot, but...the competition? That gets my brain ticking.

'Keep your mouth shut, Maggot!' snaps Jaco. 'What did the Head say? In silence, yeah.'

Maggot glares at me as if it's my fault, which it is I suppose. Then he carries on looking, but he's flushed and sullen and I can see he's not really paying attention to what he's doing. He just wants to move on, get it finished. He picks up the maths book, opens it in the middle, and then lets it drop.

Yes! Missed it!

But even he can't miss my stick mirror; I can see the end of it poking out from under the last couple of exercise books at the bottom of the desk.

I force myself to look away. I yawn and start to

hum.

'Shut up, Trokka.'

I stop humming.

What could any of us have that would be to do with the competition? A list? A form? A newspaper cutting? A note? Note! Am I stupid or what? I stick my hands in my pockets and discreetly scrumple up the scrap of paper until it's a little ball between my thumb and forefinger, easy enough to flick away. But why would the Serpent be looking for a note, looking for anything? Because he suspects something, or someone rather, someone who is onto him, someone who isn't quite as crushed as all the other poor mugs who've no choice but to walk the hill to the Serpent's school. Well, he's right there. We're not and I think the false fire alarm spooked him and seeing me down on that second level – except he clearly didn't know who it was – and that must have spooked him more. No one in the school has ever said anything about the second level. Never even knew it existed. His big secret. Except there's a bigger, nastier secret down there. I'm sure of it, and we're going to find out what it is. It's almost out of the bag, and then you, Sir Pent, can be the one who is stuffed, tied in a knot and left to rot.

Maggot looks up from my desk and his eyes

narrow suspiciously. 'What you got to grin about, Trokka? Do you think I'm stupid or something?'

'No.'

'No is right.' He lifts up the last of the books and my heart sinks. 'And what's this then?' He's got the spy stick in his hand and he's frowning at it.

I shrug. 'I want to be a dentist. You've seen what they use?' Stupid question, the Maggot is more likely to invent time travel than he is to brush his teeth.

'Yeah,' he says doubtfully.

'Let me show you,' I say, 'it's like this,' making to take it from him but he snatches it away.

'Oi, none of that...Jaco, look at this!'

But miracle of miracles, my bacon is saved because at that moment Blake, Mr Supergeek himself, sails in and does he look weird! Arsenal fan meets Guy Fawkes rocket: shimmery red-and-black stripy T-shirt, a white sweat band round his wrist, orange skater trousers with the bum hanging almost to his knees, and bright green runners.

Everybody gawps, even Dorner looks up from his newspaper, and then blinks.

'Oh yes!' exclaims Blake, 'Eggy hunt!' a dim grin spreading across his wide face. Then he does the high-pitched cackle thing that passes for a laugh. What a goon! But if there was a competition for getting noticed, he would carry off the prize, no bother.

The class begins to titter and that kind of scared tense feeling that Jaco just loves to create eases a bit. Jaco stops what he's doing. 'Where've you been, Blake?'

Blake starts to tell us all about his sick auntie and how he had to go and visit her and it's the lamest excuse for a bunk-off that any of us have ever heard. But Maggot is so spellbound he doesn't notice me gently taking the spy stick out of his hand and slipping it back into my desk. Bacon well and truly saved; thank you, Blake.

Even Jaco can't help giving a smile. 'All right, shut it and sit down,' he says. 'We don't want your life history.' Then to Mr Dorner: 'We've finished, Mr Dorner.'

Jaco goes out, I suppose to report to Robestone. The two other Bins go back to their places and Mr Dorner folds up his paper and goes back to Ancient Greece – down into the underworld again – everyone going somewhere; everyone but us.

I slip the Pimpernel's note out of my pocket and carefully smooth it out. Mr Dorner's voice murmurs on with lists of names that sound a bit like mine, which is oddly comforting, not that I'm listening; my eyes are on the spidery writing:

'They're alive and they're in the country.'

'They' – the winners! – and the Pimpernel knows! How? What does it matter? He's the Pimpernel! Newspapers and telly know nothing; *he* knows. They haven't been spirited away to the bottom of the sea or into Dorner's Hades – they're here somewhere and we can find them. I look over at Charlie's desk and I catch myself beginning to grin.

'Patroclus, take that stupid smile off your face.'

'Yes, Sir.'

A few of my classmates give me weird looks, but I don't care. Sir Pent and Robestone and the bullying Bins think that they can push us around and do what they want, but they don't know about us, about the Geek and me and how we've fooled them. And they don't know about the Pimpernel – and that is the biggest thing they don't know.

It's not just that he is Mr Mystery, Mr Everywhere when you don't expect him; but he's seven steps ahead of the game. Seven steps ahead of us too: gasman, fireman, he's as smart and tricky as a chess champion, as the geezer who thought up the wooden horse to get into Troy. And he's picked us.

But who is he? Maybe he's not in the school at all. Someone from outside then? Maybe he works for a newspaper and has a network of helpers, a gang of people right across the country that he can call on, like the gasman, or the fireman. And now us, me and the Geek. So we're part of something really big, really important. And we've done OK and we've got something to tell him when he makes contact again.

One: the Serpent has a secret.

Two: the secret is kept down on the second level.

Three: that competition was a fake. The Serpent hates clever students but he likes Staleways getting high up in all those exam lists.

But there's also a four and a five that I'm not so sure about.

Four: we need to get into his office because there has to be some clue there.

Five: breaking into the school in the middle of the night is going to be scary, but that's what we have to do.

And I wonder how the Pimpernel will make contact this time?

Chapter 20

I'm the other side of the road from the school gates, watching as the last of the pupils stream by me and start heading down the hill towards the town. I've got my bag on the pavement, half unpacked, as if I'm checking to see if I've left something behind, but in fact, I'm really looking at the building carefully, really carefully, because I realise in all these years I've never really studied it. Never wanted to. Always kept my head down going up the hill; and got my back to it when I'm going home. Only time I see it is when I get bad dreams and it's sitting there, on the top of the hill, like a rest home for vampires.

Out comes the last pupil; it's the Geek. Robestone's at the entrance but she walks past him without looking his way and as soon as she's through, he starts to swing his side of the big iron gate across. He sees me and glares suspiciously but I pretend not to notice either him or the Geek, who hurries by like she's got a bus to catch, except no buses come up the hill.

'Seven o'clock at my place,' I say, stuffing the last of my books back in my bag.

'I'll be there.' She says as she walks past me.

The second half of the gate swings shut with a clang and I stand up. The gate's the only way in: the wall's too high and there's nothing to scramble up. But the gate, if we use a rope, might be possible, though I don't like the look of the spikes at the top. Then what?

The main building sticks up from behind the iron gates, its walls the colour of dirty laundry, thin windows and heavy black drainpipes coming down from a roof that's as steep and pointy as a witch's hat. That's where the Pent House is, right high up. If we come up here late, we can watch and see if his lights go on or not; if not, that will be the go-ahead signal for us. But we still have to find a way into the main building because it'll be locked up tight as a drum after our false fire alarm.

I pick up my bag and sling it on my shoulder; I can't hang around for ever. Even if I can't see anyone watching me, you don't know do you, from one of those windows, maybe there's Robestone or one of the others. It makes me feel prickly and nervous. I start to make my way down the hill.

School? It's a prison: when you're in you can't get out; when you're out you can't get in. But I don't give up. All the way down the hill I keep thinking, trying to picture side doors – only two: one into the kitchen and the other into the changing room. Windows we could squeeze through? None, unless we could scrabble up the wall and hang upside down like a bat.

By the time I turn into my street, I've worked out three possible ways in: one, we pick a lock (but that takes a while); two, we don't leave school at the end of the day. That means we'll have to find somewhere to hide until the whole place is quiet (but then we won't be able to see if the Serpent's lights are on. And that means we won't know whether he is up in his lair or not); three, we have to climb up the outside of the building (how can we do that?).

No prizes for my plans, then.

'Hey! Hey! Hey!' I hear their shouts at the same moment that I see them. The Bins, lounging about in the street in front of the café. What's going on?

'Trokka! Trokka! Trokka! When's the shop open for chips?'

Four of them, two leaning against the window; my dad hates that; he'll come out like a bull if he sees them, and the other two: Stef and...Blake! What's he doing in with them? It's one thing to be the class clown but can he really be that stupid to start hanging out with them in the streets. Oh well, here goes. At least there's no Jaco to really stir things up.

I don't slow down or turn away, too late for that, but I don't answer either.

'Cat got your tongue?'

'Want to get in a bin, Trokka?'

'Bet there's some greasy Greek bins round the back, Trokka.'

'It's closed,' I say. 'We don't open on Mondays.'

'Maybe you should,' says Blake, 'good for business,' and he gives his loony laugh and the others laugh with him.

Stef's ratty face leers at me. I'm getting cross and he knows it. Maggot thumps the window with the palm of his hand. 'Maybe your dada's having a kip.'

'Maybe we ought to chuck a brick through the window.'

'Do and I'll call the police.'

'Oh yeah, your word against ours.'

At that moment, a car speeds down the road and

the boys all take a step back. The car drives on but in its wake I hear the sound of a bike rattling over the bad surface of the road. I can't turn because Maggot and his mate have pushed themselves away from the window and towards me; Stef has grabbed a fist-sized stone and is jigging it up and down in his hand.

'Go for it Stef,' says Maggot. 'Maybe Mr Pimpy'll come and save Trokka. Maybe Trokka is Mr Pimpy and he'll save himself. What about that then!'

Blake giggles.

Stef's arm swings back.

The bike doesn't rattle on down the street as I expect but squeals to a stop, and there's a click and a flash.

'Oi!'

'Perfect.'

The Geek!

'Are you going to put it through the window or not?' she asks. 'It'll make an even better shot for the local paper.'

And so matter of fact you would think she was just doing her homework.

They gawp at her. They gawp at the camera she's got pointing at them and then Stef drops the stone.

'Don't be daft,' he grumbles. 'We was only

messin'.'

The Geek has swung the bike round. Good for her, ready to speed off if they go for her, but they don't. Like dogs, they begin to slink off. Blake first. I bet he wouldn't like his picture in the local; Daddy wouldn't be pleased at all.

'You watch it, Trokka,' says Stef, jabbing his finger at me. 'We got your number, so you watch it.'

I don't trust myself to say anything smart – I feel all tense and a bit shaky, so I keep my mouth shut. I don't even look at the Geek, just keep my eyes on them, sloping off, kicking a bottle so it goes skittering across the road and smashes into little pieces on the far kerb. There's a shout and a laugh and another shout that sounds like they're yelling 'Blake' and then they're round the corner into the next street, Tiller Row. Maggot lives there with his nan. Poor nan.

'Good timing. How did you know to bring a camera?'

'What are you talking about?'

I give her a blank look.

'You called me, told me to!'

'I didn't. Didn't even know you had a camera.'

The penny drops.

'The Pimpernel?' she says quietly, like someone

on this empty street might be listening.

'Must be!'

Woah! I think, this guy can think round corners.

'You sure it wasn't you, Patroclus? It sounded just like you and I called you by your name and you didn't say it wasn't you.'

'Yeah well, I didn't know any of this was going to happen, but thanks for coming so quick. I'm going to tell Dad you saved his window from getting busted.'

'Did I? I couldn't really tell what was going on. What was weird Blake doing with them?'

'Being weird, mainly.'

We lock up the bike and go in. The place is empty, always is on a Monday: Mum and Dad are off buying the week's supplies for the café and my sister, Pia, stays late at school; she thinks she's going to be a dancer.

'Want some tea?'

'Boiled water,' she says.

'Why?'

'Good for the brain.'

'Who says?'

'It's a fact, Patroclus. Don't you know about facts? You don't have to have someone say something for it to be a fact.'

'OK. OK. It's easy to boil water but when you've got your super brain maybe you can come up with a plan for how we can get into the school.'

'I thought you'd have some ideas.'

'I did but they've all got problems.' We take our drinks up to my room.

The curtain is closed which is odd because mum usually airs my room and leaves the window open during the day, even through the winter. I switch on the light...

And there's Blake sitting in my desk chair.

It's like me and the Geek got stuck with a pin at exactly the same second.

'You!'

'Blake!'

'Hello,' says Blake.

'What are you doing in my room? And how did you get in? You've got a nerve! Why aren't you with your new mates?' I slam my door and then crossly open it again. 'You can get out,' I snap, 'Right now!'

He doesn't move a muscle and I really think I am about to go and thump him but the Geek puts a hand on my arm.

'Patroclus, wait a minute.' Then to him she says: 'You're the one who called me, aren't you?' she says to him. 'You knew what they were up to.'

He smiles. 'Of course.'

Another one great at the old 'of courses'. I feel left out here.

The Geek gives me an impatient look. 'Patroclus! Wake up. This is him!'

I can see that. 'I know who it is. I just want to know what he's doing here.'

'*Him*, Patroclus...'

And the penny drops at last. 'How could it be?'

'Because,' says Blake, taking off his fake glasses, 'I'm here – and the Pimpernel is never where you expect him. Right? Haven't you figured that much out yet?' I half expect him to give his silly laugh, but there's nothing silly about him. He's Blake but another Blake altogether. He gives us a friendly smile. 'And since you clearly didn't expect me to be here, I must be him.'

'You sound different,' I say.

'This is the real me,' he says.

Chapter 21

How does he do it? One minute he's dimmer than a twenty-five-watt light bulb and then, click your fingers and blink, and he's up in your room, cool as you like, taking charge.

'How do you do it?'

'The window, I told you. Window locks are no problem.'

'No. The fireman?' I say.

'The gasman,' says the Geek. 'And the messages.'

'In my desk.'

'In my hand!'

A quick smile crosses his face. 'I'll show you another time. It's just dressing up really; the family have always been good at it.'

I remember that room in his house, just off the office, all those clothes, was that it, his dressing up room? 'It's not just dressing up though. You're different from how you are in school.'

He leans forward slightly. 'And so, Patroclus, are you.'

'I'm not.' At least I don't think I am.

He smiles again. 'As you like...'

But then the Geek starts chucking questions at him, and I join in too.

'What do you know about Charlie and the others?'

'Are they somewhere close, do you think?'

'Are they safe?'

He holds up his hands. 'Wait a minute. First things first. What I need to know is if you and Minou meant what you wrote.'

'Meaning?'

'When we were talking online, you said you were willing to join the Pimpernel. Has anything changed your mind since then?'

'No,' the Geek doesn't even bother to look my way. 'Of course we join.' There's that 'of course' again. 'Do we have to swear an oath and stuff though?' Her glasses glint in the light. 'You know, secret things.'

'Don't be silly,' I say, 'that's just kids' stuff...'

'No, it isn't,' says Blake, 'it's exactly what I am

going to ask you to do. We're not playing games here. This is what my family does, what it has always done.'

'Dress up?' I can hear myself being sort of deliberately slow, like almost sarcastic, you know. I mean here he is, in my room, in my chair, if you don't mind, and the Geek is leaning forward, nodding to everything he says and giving me cross looks, like it's me that's done something wrong.

'No. Listen,' he says, 'don't you hate Mr Pent?' I nod. Of course I do. 'Don't you hate what he's doing? Running his school like a little prison. He can do what he likes and no one can touch him, him and his gang of deputies, Mr Robestone and then the prefects. Terrifying everyone, giving detentions to students who are doing well; and now disappearing all those winners of his competition... You know, it's people like him who take over, become leaders of a country and then really terrible things happen.'

I hadn't thought about it like this; Sir Pent taking over, turning every school in the country into a Staleways with nothing but exams and tests and bullying Bins with their red bandanas and Sir Pent becoming a member of parliament maybe, maybe prime minister, world leader – that's really scary. But I'm still feeling a bit stubborn, and I want him to tell us what he knows about the disappearing ship, and about Charlie and the others.

'OK, I don't know why he's behind this kidnap thing,' says Blake, 'but I know he is: it was his competition; he, or at least the school, arranged for the limousine to take the winners to the boat and, listen to this, the boat is owned by a company called Maximus, an international company with its head-quarters in Switzerland. And guess who's a major shareholder?'

'Sir Pent,' breathed Minou.

'Got it in one. Sir Pent, the wreathing and writhing Sir Pent.'

'But the ship vanished,' I say. 'It was in the papers, on telly, so what does it matter what connection he had with it? I mean you don't have to tell me he's bad but why lose a whole ship to kidnap some clever kids. It's just not good business.' That's the Greek part of me speaking or maybe just a family thing; Dad always talks about profit margins and percentages and my mum always laughs at him and says why do you bother to say these things, our café doesn't ever have profits or margins; and then he gets excited and says, this is it, it is our business, people come, they like our food, we like our food, and so one day we shall have profits and margins.

So there it is: I don't see what profit you can have from sinking a big ship. I look at Blake. 'Well?'

'But this is it, Patroclus. It didn't sink or vanish. It came back into harbour the next day.'

I think my brain's about to burst. 'And no one noticed? You must be kidding!'

'Different harbour, different name on the boat, but same boat...'

'How do you know?'

He looks offended. 'I saw it come in. They'd changed the name, registration, flag, everything, even the crew I think, but it was Pent's boat. No doubt about it. Where do you think I've been? What do you think I've been doing? Shopping?' He looks down at his luminous shirt and pulls a face. 'Horrible, isn't it. I've got tons of stuff even more disgusting than this. If you want to get noticed, wear shiny stuff in bright green and scarlet.'

'Why bother then?'

'A family trick.'

'To get noticed?' I'm getting confused, missing the links here, though Minou nods and smiles like he's telling us stuff she knew already and that's a bit irritating since they're both new to the school and I'm not.

'No. Wear stuff like this and you stick out like a

clown; slip back into ordinary clothes and...' he clicks his fingers, 'you disappear.'

'Like the boat.'

'You've got it. I weaselled my way on board, saw enough to tell me that though this was the boat, the winners weren't on board. The whole thing was a smokescreen: flash bulbs and rockets. Just like me! It takes everybody's eyes off what's really happening. It almost had me fooled but I asked a few questions down in the kitchens; they always know what's happening down there. They're the ones producing the food so they know the numbers. The cook told me there had been a big do for the winners in the state room and then just before they sailed, they were taken ashore, bundled into cars and driven away.

'All right, so *he's* got the winners,' says Minou. 'And we have to find out why and where.'

'I'm sure they're somewhere obvious. In the school maybe. Is that possible?'

'I don't know.' says Minou.

Then they both look at me. 'They could be,' I say. 'I'm sure he's hiding something down in the cellars, on the second level. It could be he's got them locked away down there.'

'If he has,' says Blake, 'there have to be other

people involved; he can't be bringing them food and things all the time. There are going to be guards; we'll have to nose around carefully, find out their routines.'

'I'll do that.' I say it without even thinking. 'I've been down there and I can be quiet.'

'Very good, Trokka. As I soon as I saw you, on my first day, I knew we could work together. The Pimpernel isn't one person, you know,' his eyes shine, and his expression is...I don't know how to describe it, it's like pushed forward, concentrating, looking through us to something the other side, as if he's driving down a dark road, 'it's all of us who're willing to do what has to be done to put things right, rescue anyone who's in danger; it doesn't matter where.'

'Africa?' says Minou.

'Of course. Wherever it's dangerous; it can't matter to the Pimpernel; that's always been the way: Germany in the war; my dad's father smuggled children out to Sweden; before that, he was in Spain. His father was in Turkey and before that Russia. It goes back a long way; a long long way.' He shrugs, suddenly a bit apologetic. 'Nothing special; it's just what the family does. Dad says we're programmed!'

'And they all had a gang working with them?'

'Yes, mostly. My great-grandfather was a loner. Bit of a black sheep: gambler, shady deals with some pretty nasty types in the diamond business; he lost the family fortune and then got it back again.' He pulls a face. 'I think he was a bit of a crook really; he died in the Balkans just before the First World War. Rumour was he had somehow wangled his way into the organisation that ended up killing the Archduke.' We look blank. 'Whose death started the whole war. One side of the family thinks Bertie Blake was trying to stop the murder; and the other thinks he was part of the conspiracy.'

'Not something many people would be proud of.'

He smiles. 'Maybe not, but that's who the Blakes are. Mostly good but always very very serious about what they do. So, are you with me? No one can know, ever. You understand. And it will be dangerous. It's always dangerous. Blakes have never died of old age and those who have worked alongside them run risks too.' He looks at us both, first the Geek and then me.

The Geek nods. 'We understand,' she says.

'That means whenever the Pimpernel needs help, you'll be willing.'

'Like now.'

'Yes. But it's for life. Maybe in ten years time, who knows, but can you commit to that?'

She nods and he smiles again. 'And you, Trokka?' His look is a little more appraising for me. His eyes are grey, stony grey and I realise for the first time that Blake is not someone you would want to have for an enemy. Once started on something, he would never give up. But then if you have to outsmart someone like the Serpent, that's got to be a good thing, hasn't it?

'I'm in,' I say. He's convinced me, though I think I was convinced from the moment Dorner's desk collapsed and there was the Pimpernel sign. That's when I knew we weren't entirely on our own any more. I don't even mind him calling me Trokka.

He makes us swear. No big razzamatazz, no mumbo jumbo but very serious. And as I say the words that he tells us to say I realise that there is no easy unpicking of this, the Geek and I are in something so secret we can never even tell our parents about it.

When we are finished, he sits back. 'Good,' he says, 'now the business begins. We are not just going to find the missing students; we are going to bring the whole school crashing down, and Sir Pent with it. Fear and bullying, right? That's what it's built on.'

'Yes.'

'How do we stop it?' asks the Geek.

'My job. This time anyway. Give back a little of what they dish out.' He claps his hands together. 'A few odd things happening, know what I mean? Accidents, a little bit of graffiti, the Pimpernel leaving his mark everywhere. They don't seem to like that. Wait and see.

'We'll even have Sir Pent looking over his shoulder and the Bins, in particular, are not going to be happy, especially Jaco.'

'Your mate,' I add.

He pulls a face. 'Percy Blake never knows how to pick his friends; the Pimpernel is a different sort of person altogether. And he will start work tomorrow. You two begin tonight.'

'OK.' It makes sense to break in right away. Once Sir Pent has the faintest suspicion of anyone suspecting him, he'll get rid of the evidence. That means Charlie Crocker and the others will disappear, maybe for good. 'I don't think we have much time.'

'No, Patroclus,' he agrees, 'hardly any at all. Minou tackles the study and you go down to the cellars? Am I right?'

'Yes.'

'What do you need?' he asks the Geek.

'Lightweight climbing rope, shoes with a good grip but I can probably manage in my trainers; I left a window unfastened on the first floor. I won't have too difficult a climb.'

'OK, not a problem. I'll meet you at the gate at,' he glances at his watch, 'midnight. I'll bring what you need to get in and some keys for the Serpent's door.'

'And you?' I say.

'I'm the safety net. I'll collect my goody bag, set my traps and arrange the getaway; and if either of you get into any problems, you call me with one of these.'

He gives us a little silver tube with a clip on it.

'Put it on a belt, somewhere it won't fall off. They're bleepers. Very simple. They just send a signal to each other if you twist the top. Yellow for Trokka, green for you, Minou, and mine's red. OK?' he shows how to twist the top. Simple but neat.

'OK, that's it.' He stands up and we get up too. It's funny, sort of formal. He sticks out his hand and me and Minou both shake hands with him. 'Four hours,' he says, 'midnight.' A quick smile and he sweeps back my curtain, flips up the window and in half a second he's dropped down to the yard below and he's gone.

'The only time I tried that,' I say, 'I twisted my ankle.'

'Climbing's easy,' she says. 'I'll teach you.'

A car pulls up. My parents. The Geek stays for supper and then goes home to do her homework and get ready for tonight.

'Midnight,' we both say and then just like with the Pimpernel, we shake hands.

Midnight, I can't help thinking, is when bad things happen.

Chapter 22

There's a dim yellow light on the second floor. Apart from that, the school is dark, a lumpy black shadow in the darkness. I hope the light doesn't mean someone is in there, awake, patrolling maybe. Sir Pent. One of us should have kept watch to see who left and who stayed. Too late to worry now. And I hope the window that the Geek left unlocked on the first floor is still unlocked, but most of all I wish the other two would turn up.

The plan is for the Geek to climb up to the window and then come down and let us in. If she doesn't turn up, what am I supposed to do? Turn into Spiderman? No chance.

Five long minutes tick by – it feels like forever – and then I hear the slap of running feet and panting. 'Sorry,' she says, 'fell asleep.'

Fell asleep! How could she! I spent the evening choosing what to wear and what to bring, laying it all out on my bed: black T-shirt, dark blue tracksuit bottoms, old trainers that I inked with a couple of marker pens, small torch, Blake's bleeper; and a pen knife with a million things on it that my dad bought for me and which I've never used.

'Isn't he here yet?'

'No.' I look at my watch for about the millionth time and then down the deserted street towards town, lamp posts stretched far apart and lonely in their circles of light. One minute to twelve.

Before either of us can say anything else, a quiet, drawling voice breaks the silence. 'Good, you're both wearing dark clothes.'

Startled, the Geek and I bump into each other as we spin round, trying to tell where this voice is coming from.

A shadow unpeels itself from the doorway of a house two up from where we're waiting and swiftly moves towards us. He's head to toe in black, even his hands and face. His eyes, though, gleam whitely.

'You were here all the time!'

'Dangerous to get to a rendezvous early, Patroclus. If you do, best to tuck yourself out of sight. You looked a bit, mmm, conspicuous.'

'Sorry.'

'No bother. Sir Pent turned out his lights almost an hour ago.'

That surprises me. 'He didn't leave?'

'No, but he'll be asleep by now, I expect. We'll just have to be extra quiet, that's all. Mice. You know what I mean, Trokka?'

'Yes, of course I know.'

He chuckles and slips a bag from his shoulder, pulls out a pair of trainers and hands them to Minou. 'Put these on. They'll be good for the climb.'

'Blake runners. Wow!'

'She doesn't run, you know.'

He rubs his hands together and his eyes gleam. He's loving this, you can just tell. 'We might all have to,' he says. 'Run from the devil. Are you up for it, Trokka?'

'Of course.' I think I am anyway.

'Let's go, then. Gate first.'

We slip across the road and he takes a long coil of light rope from the bag and quickly ties what looks like a rolled up towel to one end. 'It'll catch between the spikes. Padded half a broom handle so it softens the noise.' He whirls about a yard of the line weighted with the handle round his head and then lets fly. It arcs over the gate and makes a dull clump. He tugs the rope and it holds. Perfect. The Geek's first.

She wasn't joking when she said she could climb – she's up and over the spikes in two seconds.

I'm next. I do OK but the spikes aren't easy. You have to swing your foot up and then sort of lever yourself so you're poised above the points. One slip, I tell myself, and...shish kebab.

'Jump!' hisses the Geek.

I jump and land badly, grunting as I go over on my right ankle. The Geek tuts and then Blake is down and beside us. I gingerly test my weight on my foot while the other two wait. It's OK. I give a thumbs up, Blake gives my shoulder a pat and then turns and runs lightly across the open yard to the front of the school, the two of us following closely.

Blake ties a length of rope round the Geek's waist. She tests the drainpipe that runs down to the right of the door and, without a word, shins up to the ledge above the door and then gives a little jump, catches the lip of the window ledge. In one movement she's up and kneeling sideways, pressed to the glass. There's a pause. 'It's been locked,' she whispers, 'I'll have to go higher.'

'Wait. I'm coming with you.' Blake loops the rope round his waist and almost as smoothly as the Geek, he is up and over the door. I find myself holding my breath as I watch them spidering up the face of the school. Heights aren't my thing. Makes me dizzy even looking up at them.

The Geek reaches the second floor, pauses at the first window. I hear her call down: 'Locked.' Blake doesn't hesitate but moves up to join her on the ledge. There's a moment when their heads merge into one shadow. They must be deciding what to do. Come back down, I reckon. She'll end up climbing to the roof otherwise and that's not going to do her much good unless she can turn into Father Christmas and slip down the chimney.

Then she's on the move again, edging sideways; Blake, anchored behind her, paying out rope. Junior classrooms on this floor: 5B, I think. Then she's past that and onto the next. I hear the sound of a window sliding up, and then she must have untied herself because the rope suddenly swings down like a dead snake before Blake hauls it up to his ledge.

Two minutes later, the front door opens and with a little bow, Blake lets me in. 'You know what you have to do?' he whispers.

'Yes.' My job is to go down. 'How long have I got?' We didn't agree a time.

There is the flash of white teeth as he smiles. 'As

long as a piece of string,' he says. 'But if you hear any yelling, get back here double quick.' He gives my shoulder a pat. 'Find out what you can, Trokka. This is our one chance to see if they're down there somewhere. After tonight, the school will be locked up tighter than the Tower of London.'

'How do you know?'

That grin again. 'Because the Pimpernel is going to get busy! Have fun!' And he's off down the dark corridor, a little pack slung over his shoulder. His 'goody bag', he'd called it.

Fun? I hadn't thought of it like that. The stairway leading down makes me think of a mouth, a throat. I start down, slowly, carefully taking a step at a time. It's so black I can't even see my hand when I hold it in front of my face. I'm tempted to use the little pencil torch I clipped to my belt, but I don't, not yet. Not unless I really need to because going down can't be so hard. I start slow. Finger tips along the wall. Then a little more quickly. Invisible. What I'm good at.

The last step. Level One. No orange light. I creep silently along. Come to the next flight. Fingertips on the wall again, and down. Level Two. Still not a light anywhere. Maybe it was like this for Jonah in the belly of the whale, black as black and sort of suffocating. I'm so tempted to use the torch but I can't, not yet, not until I know if someone's down here, someone that Sir Pent was visiting when I spotted him – a guard maybe. And if there is, it could mean that this is where the prizewinners are. And I, the invisible Michael Patroclus could be the one to find them. But if there is a guard down here, then I've got to stay invisible and that means no torch.

The door with the number two I saw last time must be somewhere along here and I ought to check it if I can. There is a slight smell of metal and damp, and it's warm. My palms feel sticky. Yes, this is the door. I run my fingers over it, lightly, spidery. Why do I keep thinking of spiders – I hate spiders. If you look really close you can see the hair on their legs... I'm feeling for a handle. There isn't one, just a bolt. Yes! Carefully, I ease it back. It runs smoothly. Greased. That's good. Means it's used. Maybe they're the other side. Maybe this is it. OK, now the door. Just a fraction then I hold it still and listen. Nothing at all and the air smells stale. I switch on the torch and let its pencil beam move slowly round the room: shelves, stacked with papers, boxes, brown envelopes. So much for Swotshop two: just a boring storeroom. I let out my breath and click off the torch and close the door. OK, where now? Sir Pent had appeared down from the other end of the passage.

I start to edge right, hand trailing along the wall. And then there's a gap. A turning into another corridor. Cautiously I take a step and nearly pitch headfirst down another flight of stairs.

Another level! I wonder how many more there are – down and down all the way to hell. I try not to think of Mr Dorner and his Hades, gloomy halls of dripping stone, pale ghosts and some lurking monster with teeth to tear your heart out.

I take a breath and start down. I can touch both walls easily, but the stairway narrows and becomes steeper. I go more slowly, counting the steps: seventy...one hundred and ten, and eleven. 111. This is it. I hold myself as still as I can. Do I hear any sound of movement? Maybe I do. There's muffled knocks and whispering creaks. Pipes, I think, air vents. There has to be something pumping air down here. And it's so warm. Maybe there's nothing down here other than some giant boiler room.

Right or left?

Right. Keep it simple. Still no light. Here I go again. One door. Wooden. Locked. Another. Metal. Handle? Yes. Try it. Locked. The air feels like a warm wet flannel on my face. I can feel sweat on my face, and trickling down under my arms. There can't be anyone living down here, no guard. No prisoners. I tap against the metal. Too soft. I give a rap with my knuckle. It makes a flat *thunk*. I put my ear against the metal to hear if there's an answering knock. Nothing. Just the sound of blood thumping in my ears.

But there has to be something, why else would Sir Pent patrol down here? He's not interested in boilers. Another door. I listen again. Nothing. The warmth, the dark, the creepy creaking, and an awful feeling of the whole school like a gigantic black toad weighing down on the thin roof over my head, really gets to me. I begin to feel dizzy. I'm not sure which way down this black corridor I came, which door I tried last. I turn on the torch again but the corridor is so long in both directions that the skinny beam isn't strong enough to show me where they end or pick out the gap where I came down the stairs. I can feel panic begin to move in my tummy and tighten my throat.

Suddenly, I hear something over the muffled pipe noises. I listen hard and there it is again. I'm sure of it: voices. I move a couple of steps to my right and it's a bit clearer. Then it stops and I stop, waiting, holding my breath. Yes. There it is again. I put my ear to the door nearest to me. No. It's coming from above my head. On level two then? As a kind of reflex I beam the torch up across the ceiling as if it could pierce through to the next floor. Of course it doesn't do that but it picks out a tangle of cables and thick pipes, and right where the murmuring voices are coming from a square grille – air vent.

I can hear them again. Before they were indistinct, now they're clear – like the sound is coming in waves. Something to do with the way the air is being circulated maybe.

'Is it day? When's it day?'

'Go to sleep.'

'I can't. It's too bright. It's always too bright. Why don't they turn out the lights?'

'Pull the sheet over your head.'

'I can't. I can't breathe...'

And then it becomes murmuring again and then silence.

That's it! That's them! Voices of young people, not guards. Blake was right! He's got his prizewinners buttoned up tight right here! Right under everyone's nose.

I look at the grille and wonder. It's square. About eighteen inches across. Could I squeeze through that? I'm small enough. Maybe I could. Wriggle like a rat along the vent right to where they're being held. I could tell them then, tell them that help's on the way.

I try to reach the grille but it's too high. I need a chair, a box, anything to get a leg up. I try jumping and just manage to touch it, but that's stupid, bouncing up and down in a pitch black corridor like a mad kangaroo.

There's a sudden flood of light from way down to the right and a giant shadow springs along the floor towards me. I freeze, terrified, and then another voice growls down at me from the grille: 'Shut up will you, or I'll have your guts for my dog. All right? You understand me, do you?' For half a second I think it's me he's talking to but that's stupid – it's the prisoners and he's their guard.

The shadow slips away but the light's still there.

I jolt into action. That guard only has to step out and look this way and I'm meat. I nip into a doorway and press myself against the door.

A door clicks. Footsteps coming this way. Run or don't run? The options click up double fast. One: if I run I've a good chance of getting away but then they'll know something's up and they won't take any risks; they'll move the students somewhere else, or worse, get rid of the evidence – get rid of them. Two: if I run there will be an alarm and Blake and Minou

might be stuck hanging from a drainpipe somewhere and get caught and they'll be got rid of.
Three: this is three. I squeeze my eyes tight and
flatten myself even more. I'm an omelette, I tell
myself, a skim of paint... I can hear his raspy
breathing and smell stale beer and sweat.

I'm invisible, I tell myself. But I don't feel invisible.
I feel huge and lumpy and obvious, and any second
I expect to get hauled out into the open, hands
round my throat, ear gripped and twisted...

And then the footsteps are going away. I open my
eyes just in time to see a shape disappearing round
a corner, the shadow jumping after. The light goes
and I'm back in the thick black darkness again.

And now I really move. I've got to have at least
one of the others to hoick me up to that grille but
where are they right now? Use the bleeper,
Patroclus. I do, and then I get a move on, up to our
meeting place in the entrance hall.

No feeling my way this time; on with the torch
and run. Find the first set of narrow stairs and I'm
up them, all one hundred and eleven, in seconds.
Left. Along. Up again. Left. Along. Up again. My
chest is burning, eyes watering. I reach the main hall
and stagger right into Blake.

Chapter 23

'Steady on,' Blake says. 'Take a breath and then tell me quick as you can what the story is.'

He's brisk, businesslike.

I do as he says and as I'm telling him, the Geek joins us, trotting down the main stairs as if she owns the place. Look at us now, I can't help thinking, if the police walked in, they'd take us for a gang of thieves, lock us up tighter than Sir Pent ever would.

'Didn't see you? Are you sure? Good.' Then he turns to the Geek. 'Minou, you stay up here. Don't touch anything, especially not the light switch to these stairs.' A quick smile. 'Don't ask, you'll find out tomorrow. Trokka and I will be back in ten minutes. If we're not, you go.'

'The rope on the gate,' she says. 'Do you want me to leave that?'

'Yes.'

Then we're off, me leading the way, Blake right on my heels. He's so quiet I almost think there's no one there but when I stop and half turn to check, I feel the touch of his hand on my shoulder, urging me on.

Down we go – another level. Then the narrow stairs, and we're in level three. I slow down, count the doorways. No light up ahead, no sound of voices, only the pipes, just like before. I click on the torch and pick out the grille to show Blake.

'If you get on my shoulders,' he whispers, 'do you think you could unfasten it?'

'Yes. You'll need to shine a light up there though, so I can see. It's screws I think.'

'No problem.' He hands me a fist-sized power screwdriver. 'This'll do. Don't lose the screws and just remove the grille and then we'll decide on stage two.'

I scramble onto his shoulders; he's steady as a rock and I remember the way Stefan tried to claim he'd been mugged and dumped by a gang. It was never a gang, just Blake. In two ticks I have the four screws out and the grille in my hand. He passes me the torch and I shine it down the vent – a passage, same size as the grille, that runs above the corridor ceiling. I can see a couple of shafts leading left and right.

'What do you think, Trokka? Is it possible?' he whispers. 'Could I crawl down it?'

'No, but I think I could. Is that stage two?'

'Of course. Find the room they're being kept in, Trokka, and tell them the Pimpernel's on his way.'

'Is that all?'

'Keep your face out of sight.'

'Charlie might recognise my voice.'

'Even so – he can suspect just so long as he doesn't know for sure. It's better that way. All right?'

'Yes.'

'Up you go then.' He gives me a heave and I catch the lip of the opening with both hands and haul myself up. For a second, my feet are dangling in the air, then he catches them and gives me a shove and I'm up and in. Possible? Yes, but not too much turning room; I'll just have to squeeze down. Toothpaste. I'm pretty sure I have a rule about not being toothpaste.

I begin my journey.

If the corridor was bad this is ten times worse, but if something has to be done, no point putting it off.

Elbows and knees inching along, back rubbing on the top, every sound amplified. Even my breath sounds like a hurricane in my ears.

But then I hear the voices again. Whispering. And there's a light up ahead, though it doesn't seem to be coming from the end of the shaft, from a side one then. Corners? How am I to get round corners?

I reach the branch: sharp right turn. I can't do it, not by kneeling. I try and push, the corner cuts into me. I just can't do that shape. The sweat is dripping in blobs from my nose but I can't get my hand back to wipe it. I close my eyes and picture myself in this shaft, as if I were a drawing for an experiment. And then I have it! So simple. I stretch out flat, arms out in front of me and lie on my side and then ease myself round the corner. It's not long before I'm over the room.

At first I can't see much: a table, floor, all white, cut up into the little black squares of the grille. Then an arm and a voice, whispering again.

'I heard something.'

A girl's voice answers. 'Go to sleep, please, just go to sleep. He'll only come in if he hears us and you know what he threatened. And if Mags wakes she'll start crying. She's frightened he'll switch on the bands and we'll have to work all night then.'

Don't know what she means by the bands but the first voice was Charlie Parker. I am one hundred per cent certain of that.

'But I heard something. I'm telling you. Up there.'

'Probably a rat.'

That's me. Better a rat than toothpaste, I suppose. Time to say hello. 'Hssst!'

'That's not a rat!'

'Up here!'

'It's someone!'

'Are you sure?'

A face at the grill, peering up. Charlie. And then a second one, a girl.

'What are you doing? Who are you? If they catch you...'

'I'm with the Pimpernel; we've been looking for you. Don't worry, we'll get you out.' I sound confident – at least I think I do – but here I am squished in an air vent and I haven't got a clue how we'll get them past the guard.

'Shh, you must keep quiet, please.' It's the girl.

Charlie ignores her: 'Pimpernel?' He squints and I know he is trying to peer into the darkness and see who I am but he can't. 'He really exists then?' And then over his shoulder, 'I'll tell you later,' he says to the girl, who's wanting to know what we're talking about. 'They're making us take exams. Tests. I don't know. All the time. On computers. It never stops.'

Another Swotshop! Swotshop 3. Meaningless slogging tests. What is Pent's game?

The girl's face is close to the grille now. She's one of the winners I saw on television. 'How are you going to get us out?' she says.

Good question.

'A plan.'

'I'm not crawling along pipes; I won't fit.'

'She won't,' says Charlie. 'She's huge.'

'I'm not huge. I'm just not skinny.'

This could go on all night and my elbows are sore and I'm wondering whether I'm going to manage going backwards. Not much choice.

'When?' says the girl.

'Soon. Be ready.'

'What do you mean, be ready? We can't do anything. They never let us out at all.'

Why's she sounding so cross? It's not like it's my fault. 'I said we'd get you out. You work in that room too?'

'Yes.' It's Charlie again. 'Don't mind her; she's all right really. Worried though, about her mum. She's only got a mum. They'll all be worried won't they, all our families...'

There's a bang on their door – a fist thumping angrily.

'Him!' The girl pushes Charlie to one side and hisses at me. 'He can hear us. Go but be really quiet.'

I'll hardly be singing the national anthem.

Then, as I am beginning to experiment with my reverse gear, she adds: 'Tell everyone we're here. The police, everyone.'

'Sure. Don't worry.'

I hear the door to their room slam open and see a burly shape striding past right under me. A sweaty bald head and inky blue veins pumped up at his temples.

'Which one of you's talking again? I warned you, right?' His voice is slurred, stretchy as a rubber band.

'Can't we even whisper? I can't sleep and it helps if I can just whisper.'

'You can't even twitch a mushcle unless I shay sho. And I'm not inclined...to shay sho. You gorrat? No one shees you down here, no one; sho if you want me to put you through a mangle no one's going to know. Know what I mean?' I get a reek of beer wafting up to me.

A very quiet 'yes' from the girl.

I'm not twitching a muscle. I'm not even breathing. He's standing so close to me that if the grille wasn't there I could reach out and touch that blue vein throbbing on the side of his waxy bald head. He stands still for a moment, not saying anything but breathing heavily through his nose. For some reason he makes me think of the one-eyed giant, the cyclops, guarding his cave – eating his prisoners one by one. Does he sense me?

Over and over again, I'm saying to myself: don't look, Mr Cyclops. Don't you look round.

Then he grunts: 'Don't expect breakfast to-morrow,' and he sways over to the door, and slams it shut after him. I start moving backwards. I can do it. I sort of dig with my toes and push with my elbows and slide, a couple of inches at a time. It takes ages but I reach the junction and remember to go on my other side so I'm facing the right way and then it's the long straight wriggle. No light to guide me this time though, blind as a mole I am. When I reach the vent where we took the grille out I almost fall through.

How am I going to get down? Head first is the answer. No option. 'Blake?'

'Don't worry, I'll catch you.' His voice comes calmly out of the darkness. Weird the way he's just so matter of fact about all this stuff. He makes me think of a doctor or chemist or something.

I push myself over the edge and hang the top half of my body down and he takes me under the arms and keeps me upright as my legs slide out after me, slapping noisily against the floor. We both freeze and then he touches my arm and I replace the grille, then we go, hurrying back up to the main hall where the Geek is waiting.

Chapter 24

'Should we go back and get them now?'

It's two o'clock in the morning. We're back in my room, as it's the closest to the school. Climbed in through the same window Blake used earlier. The family are all asleep but I feel wired up like a light bulb. Sir Pent's a criminal, a kidnapper, and we can prove it! We've stolen our way into the school, right under the nose of his guard, and got away with it. That's really something.

I've made hot chocolate and both Blake and the Geek have the mugs cradled in their hands and are taking sips. 'Good chocolate, Trokka.'

For a second, him saying that made me think of Jaco. The Geek never calls me Trokka but she's very particular, the Geek, likes things just so, wanted an extra half lump of sugar in her chocolate. Who has sugar in hot chocolate anyway! She was pretty impressed with my finding the missing winners, though – especially me climbing into the vent. She said that was 'intrepid' – a geek word if ever there was one. But she's the cool one, up the side of the school like it was a kids' climbing frame and then scoping Pent's office without batting an eyelid. And now I feel we should get it over and done with. Get them out. 'So what do you think, Blake?

'Well,' he says slowly, 'have you worked out how we're going to get past the guard?'

'No, it's just I think we should strike when the kettle...'

'Iron,' corrects the Geek, 'when the iron is hot, Patroclus.'

'Yes, you know what I mean.'

'Sure,' says Blake, 'but let's hear what Minou found out first, OK?'

The Geek puts down her mug and tucks her knees up under her. 'I went through all his papers. He's very organised so it was easy. There was stacks of stuff – memos, notes in his diary. I even checked through his emails. He knows everyone, you know, even the prime minister.' She opens a folder. 'I photocopied some of the papers for evidence and made notes from the rest.' She looks at us both. 'He intends to take over everything. Start small, you know, special adviser to the minister of education and then wiggle his way up. It's what we thought.'

Sir Pent coiled around the country, scenting out profit, squeezing the life and colour out of everything. We won't be mice, but ghosts.

'And this competition,' says Blake, 'is the first step?'

'Yes. The winners are his meal ticket; they're going to make the school famous. I found out what the Swotshops are really for; not just punishment. He's programmed a computer to produce every possible exam question in every subject. Can you imagine? That's thousands and thousands and thousands of questions. The tests me and Patroclus had to do on Saturday are like the easier ones, OK. To cover all the really tricky questions, he needed to get the best brains in the country; that's what his competition was for and why the winners suddenly disappeared and are now down where you found them, Patroclus.'

'Swotshop three.'

'Exactly.'

But there's something stupid about it. 'If he uses computers to make up loads of questions, why can't he use them to make up the answers?'

Blake's eyes had been fixed on the Geek, like he was weighing every word she said, now he glances up at me. 'Why do you expect people like him to make sense, Trokka?'

'Because he's into profit, isn't he? This doesn't make business sense, that's all.'

'I know exactly why he's doing this,' says the Geek primly. 'A computer will give all the computer-right answers to any set question. It can't do all the little unexpected variations you're going to get from really clever people. That's what he's got in his notes anyway. And you know what, Patroclus? He wanted you and me to do the competition, wanted to stuff us down in that Swotshop too – reckons we're top brains! How about that!' She smiles for the first time.

'And that,' says Blake, 'is why you're both with me.'

So it's a geek revolution, I think. One in the eye for the Bins and anyone who thinks like them. It makes me feel good.

'And I'll tell you something else,' she says, 'it's why the Bins are with Sir Pent. Did you know that all the Bins that leave this school are now getting top level in every subject? That's top marks in the country. He's cracked the system so that whatever exam they sit he can feed them in one of his ready-made answers; it's just straightforward cheating really. Staleways is set to be top of the league tables, so that means he'll get his post as adviser, no problem. Step one, get it.' She takes a deep breath. 'And there's a bonus this time. He, or at least the school, is in the running for a massive grant. Do you want to know how much?'

'Go on,' says Blake.

'One million pounds.'

One of us whistles. I think it's me. 'And he's going to spend it on the school?'

'I don't think so,' she says in that up and down TV way that means, stupid question. 'I found details of a bank account on the Channel Islands.'

'A little nest egg,' says Blake. 'And the Bins are going to be his own private army. It seems like he's got it all thought out. Nothing to get in his way to the top...nothing but us, that is.' He gives his weird laugh. This time the Geek and me join in, but maybe not quite so hysterically as Blake.

'Is that a real laugh?' I ask him when he's dabbed his eyes and quietened down, 'or just one you put on for a...laugh, when you're being the other you.'

'It's me. Sorry. The Blakes laugh that way, always have I think. My dad has it worse than me.'

'I haven't finished,' says the Geek. 'When I checked his diary, he'd written, *Minister to visit school. Prepare special show.*'

'When's that?'

'Tomorrow.' She puts down her mug of chocolate and folds her arms. 'That's my report.'

'Thank you, Minou.' Blake sounds as balanced and calm as ever but his eyes are sparkling. 'You may well be the Pimpernel's best pair of eyes - you did a thorough scout. You both did and now we're going to have real fun.'

'When?'

'Tomorrow, of course, when the Minister visits. Sir Pent is bound to make loads of speeches in the hall – that will be the 'special show'. Now, I've left a few Pimpernel specials around and about the place; they were just intended to stir things up and rattle his cage but now we are going to have to do more than that,' he says, rubbing his hands together. 'Because the Minister is there, the press will be, too. Fantabulous, my friends, I feel very, very merry. This is going to be Sir Pent's big exit and with any luck it will be on television. Now, let's plan. When will be the best time to get down to Swotshop Three?'

'When everyone's in the hall,' I say.

'Good.'

'Everyone but us,' adds the Geek.

'And our guard, Trokka's bald Cyclops, he likes his drink, you reckon.'

'He stank of it,' I say.

'Then I think he might find it hard to resist a bottle of my great-great-grandfather's Napoleon brandy. Into which I shall pop a couple of my mother's sleeping pills. They take about two hours to kick in, at least they did when I tried them.'

'You can't sleep!'

'Sleep like a log. I was just testing them. Knew they would come in handy. I'll do an early morning delivery down to level three – leave it at the door to the Swotshop with a little thank-you note from Sir Pent himself. It doesn't sound like our guard will be too fussy about checking. So, plan one is simple: once our friend is snoring, it shouldn't be too hard to unlock the door and let them out. There'll be some press in the hall but a TV crew would be better still, positioned at the gate. I think a couple of phone calls are in order.'

'You can arrange that?' The Geek is impressed.

'Pimpernel strings.' He laughs. 'It's a family thing. Now, I'll fix it that Pent's big moment in the Hall turns into total chaos. At that point you two have got to slip out and make your way down to the third level.'

We talk through the details and at the end Blake says: 'I think that the three of us should be able to manage him. Don't you agree?' Of course, Blake hasn't seen Cyclops.

The Geek, who hasn't seen Cyclops either, says yes. I say yes too but I can't say I feel one hundred per cent confident.

'It's easy after that: we go straight to the waiting TV cameras. Bingo!'

'What about us?'

'Rear guard,' says Blake. 'In case the plan doesn't quite...' he waves his hands, 'you know. And, well I didn't say this before, but the Pimpernel has a thing about the press and publicity. It's good for the name to be known, but not us; we stay invisible. Simple eye masks will do – I'll provide them.'

'Live to fight another day,' I suggest.

'That sort of thing.' He stands up. 'Don't be surprised if you don't see me in school first thing tomorrow. And don't worry, Trokka, my old mate, I shall be the fun!' He laughs when he sees our horrified expressions because for one second he sounded exactly, *exactly* like Jaco. Then he straightens himself a little and pushes his hand through his hair just like Sir Pent does. 'School,' he breathes in a whispery voice, 'I have some exciting news...' and I swear by all that is holy he's oozy Mr Pent. The Geek claps her hands with delight, I think my mouth is hanging open so I close it. 'And the news is...' his voice and everything else about him becomes Blake again... 'the Serpent will be tied in a knot so tight he'll find it hard to breathe.'

'How do you do that?'

'Years of practice.'

'Told you, the Pimpernel has to be everywhere but he can never be himself. Only you two know – you two and my dad.'

'Not your mother?' says the Geek.

'No. She'd worry too much. Remember your oath – you tell no one, no family, not even your pet gerbil.'

I look at the Geek. 'I don't have a gerbil,' she says primly.

'If you say so, Minou.' He smiles and stands up. 'The Pimpernel will see you both tomorrow.' Odd the way he sometimes does that, refers to the Pimpernel as if he were someone else. Then he lifts his hand in a half-salute, half-goodbye and swings his legs over the windowsill and drops silently down into the yard below.

The Geek takes off her glasses and gives them a

polish. 'I don't know why he said that.'

'What?' I'm thinking that he hasn't said very much at all.

'About the gerbil.'

'That? Forget it, it was just a joke.'

'But,' she says, 'I do have a gerbil.'

'Then why did you make such a big thing about saying you didn't? I don't understand.'

'Because I didn't know if he was guessing or if actually knew. How could he know, Patroclus? I mean I like him,' she says. 'At least, I think I like him; but I don't feel I know him. We still don't know very much about him and yet he seems to know all about us.'

'I suppose that to be the Pimpernel, you have to know everything; even if it means finding out about your friends.'

She pulls a face, not convinced.

'Anyway, of course you like him, you wouldn't have joined if you didn't...' I know even as I am saying this that it isn't a question of liking, it is more to do with trust and sharing something, a strong feeling of what's right, maybe. I don't know. I'm tired and wish the Geek would go home. Tomorrow is going to be a battle and I'm hoping I don't do anything wrong and spoil things. And anyway I do like Blake. I like his weirdness and the way he laughs and the way he can do voices. I bet that's what he'll do tomorrow – of course it is. He'll do voices and fool them all.

'Yes, he's really funny, isn't he? I like that.' She gets up. 'Meet you at the corner tomorrow, usual time?'

'Yes.'

'Do you think there'll be a reward? My mum could do with a reward.'

'I don't think so. It's not why we're doing it, is it?'

'No. I suppose you're right. You're a good thinker, Patroclus, aren't you?' She gives me a look. 'Do you mind if I don't climb out of the window? I think I would prefer to use the front door. I'll be quiet as a mouse.'

Mouse? I don't think we're the mice any more.

I see her out and as I slowly go up the stairs to my bedroom I am trying to think what I can use to hit the cyclops over the head – something like a handle, maybe wrapped in an old shirt, sort of padded but hard. My father is snoring as I pass his bedroom door.

Chapter 25

My mother is singing quietly when I come into the kitchen to have breakfast. My father is sitting at the table reading the paper and frowning. It doesn't mean anything that he's frowning; it's just what he does when he reads.

'Michael! *Kali mara*, boy. Last night I dreamed of islands; the sea was so blue. I had never seen it such a colour in all my life. Can you imagine that?'

I kiss my mother and kiss my father. Outside the sky is grey. 'We did ancient Greece in class yesterday,' I tell him. 'Hades and all that stuff.'

'What do you mean "stuff"? You should show respect, Michael. These stories are what it means to be Greek. Not like this!' He slaps the paper; the local paper. 'The headlines are all about the ministerial visit to the school. Why to the school, I ask, and all these children gone. Pouf.' He snaps his fingers. 'Like this. Nothing. These are all the stories we have now; little nothings. No great men, no heroes.' He waves his hands, 'No giants.'

My mother tells him to stop getting excited and start doing some work. I think of Cyclops but I don't disagree with my father. One, because it is never a good idea to disagree with him too much; he gets upset and very noisy. Two, because I need to get going. And three, I can't tell him that he's wrong; there is a good story about the visit, a story that must finish today.

I meet the Geek at the usual corner and we head up the hill together. I stop and buy a couple of bars of chocolate and give one to her. 'In case Jaco or one of the others stops us. We don't need them searching us today.'

'I don't have anything for them to find. Do you?'

'Yes.' What I have in my backpack is my big deal. It's what was keeping me awake last night, my club that I'm going to have to whack the Cyclops with.

'What is it?'

'If I tell you, you're not to laugh.'

'OK.'

'Well, what would you use to make a club?'

She thinks for a second. 'Easy – a rolling pin.

Maybe a rounders bat if I had one, but I don't. So?'

'I didn't have rounders bat either.'

'Patroclus, you have a rolling pin in your bag, is that it?'

'Yes. No big deal. I've taped a hand towel round it.'

'Impressive. My father wouldn't know what a rolling pin is.'

I'm surprised. That's the first time I've ever heard her mention her dad. I sort of had the feeling she lived alone with her mum. I suppose I never asked and she never said. 'My father's a cook,' I tell her, 'so's my mother; of course I know about kitchens.'

'I don't know what my father does.' She says it like she's got zero interest in him so instead we talk about what kind of Pimpernel traps Blake has set. He wouldn't tell us last night, said he didn't want 'to give the game away'. I think he wants to surprise us as much as Sir Pent.

There's a small group of Bins hanging around the gates when we get there, which is odd because it's rare for anyone to be ahead of me coming into school. But there they are, Stef, Maggot, and the two sullen brothers. Stef's eyes light up when he sees us together.

'Oh lovey dovey,' he coos. 'Oh it's the pally wally

spods coming to school together.'

And there's something about his rat face and stupid sneering that gets to me. 'What are you doing here, Stef?' I say. 'I thought you liked it round by the kitchens, sticking your nose in the bins.'

He flushes. 'Don't get smart, Trokka.' He pokes a finger in my chest and I take half a step backwards.

Smart alecs get binned straight off. Why didn't I keep my mouth shut?

'Pally wally,' he repeats. Giving me another poke. 'Lovey dovey, right?' The other three crowd round me. It's time to back track and change gear. Play the game, Patroclus, one last time. 'Right,' I say.

'And did you buy her some flowers?' says Maggot.

'Not yet.'

I sense the Geek is ready to explode but I can't afford even to give a warning look - that would be asking for trouble.

'Pansies?' says Maggot. They all laugh. Then, here it comes: 'Got some chocca, Trokka?' and Stef flips up my pocket and lifts out the bar I put there just for this purpose. 'Good man,' he says in a stupid attempt at a posh voice. 'Very decent. Most obliged. Ta-ra, then?'

I shove my way through the group of them; they

make a point of not getting out of the way but they let The Geek through easy. I don't know but I think she's developing a pretty scary stare through those glasses of hers – what they call 'the evil'. Not bad.

'Sorry,' I say, when I catch up with her. 'Should have kept my mouth shut.'

'What's to be sorry for? Today's their last day,' and she gives a laugh and I don't know why but that makes me laugh too. I look back over my shoulder and the Bins are staring at us. They're not used to swots being happy just after a mugging. And I know this is going to be a good day. A Pimpernel day.

Robestone is on the front steps. He scowls his morning scowl and tells us to go straight to the classroom.

I bet he saw his Bins doing their usual morning bullying, would probably like to join in. 'Have a nice day, sir,' I say.

'Mind your tongue, Patroclus!'

It doesn't matter what you say to him, he thinks you're being cheeky. I mean I could say, here's a cheque for a million pounds and he'd probably put me in the Swotshop. If he hopes he's getting any of that million-pound grant for himself, he's got another think coming.

No traps visible in the hall, nothing in the main

corridor and nothing in the classroom either. But I bet they're there. I wonder what will happen when someone turns the light switch on. I whistle quietly to myself as I hang up my bag in the changing room so I can pick it up later, and then go into class.

Morning assembly we get the big talk. 'Best behaviour, school, as always.' The usual oily cheesy stuff from Mr Gold-and-Silver; he's got even more jewellery on today than usual and he's wearing a dark-red velvet suit. The Geek said it was burgundy. It made me think of blood.

He tells us about how we are privileged today and I suppose he is going to tell us about this minister and the press and all that, but he never gets to finish his sentence. His oozy-looking face suddenly twists up into an expression of surprise and twitchy discomfort; and he's like a puppet and someone else is jerking the strings. He shivers and jigs about in his suit and then starts to scratch himself like there's no tomorrow. Monkeys in the zoo wouldn't have a patch on him. He's got one arm round his neck and halfway down his back, and he's bent down scratching his ankle with the other.

There is silence in the hall; you could hear a pin drop, except it isn't a pin that we're hearing but his scratching. He pulls himself together and starts again: 'Tremendous privilege to have...' and then he's at it again. Must be an agony of itching. This time someone begins to snigger.

Robestone snaps: 'Silence! Who is that boy? You...' But others have started now and Robestone realises that he's onto a loser here so he steps up to the front of the dais, mutters something to the writhing Serpent and then barks out: 'School dismissed. Back to class. This instant!' And out we go.

I look back and see the Serpent being helped down from the dais. Bins are on either side of the door, staring at us, pulling out anyone grinning, anyone who might possibly be guilty. My face is blank. I'm good at looking like there's nothing going on because I practise by imagining a turned off TV screen, works every time. What I'm thinking though is: 'Itching powder of some sort. Simple yet highly effective. That's one for Blake.' I'm careful not to catch the Geek's eyes. It wouldn't do for them to link us to this in some way. That wouldn't do at all.

Blake's second gag is waiting for us out in the main hall. How did he manage it, because there was no sign of it on the way in, but there it is, a huge scarlet banner stretched right the way across from one wall to the other with 'Let them go' written across it and then the Pimpernel's logo in shiny black under the words.

Everyone's buzzing.

'What's that mean?'

'I dunno.'

'We've seen that squiggle before, haven't we?'

'Pimpernel,' I say. 'It's the Pimpernel.'

'Yeah, brilliant,' mutters the boy next to me as we are going through to the corridor. 'He done a joke in your class, collapsed desk.'

'Yes.'

'Do you think he done the headmaster? Made him scratch?'

'Could be.'

'Brilliant.'

'No talking! Straight to class!'

Jaco's at the door. 'What do you know about all this, Trokka?' he says to me as I'm going in. 'It was a bit of a laugh wasn't it, don't you think?'

He doesn't fool me. Expect me to tell him anything! He must be joking. 'Did the Bins do it, then? You and them?'

He gives me a sharp punch in the tummy that makes me go 'Whoof!' and double over. 'Don't try it on, Trokka, my old mate. And just remember if you hear anything, you tell me. That goes for you all, you dumb nerds,' he says to the rest of the class. 'Anyone caught with anything, anything at all that links them to that berk who's stupid enough to call himself a flower is going to wish he'd never been born. I mean it.'

Jaco would enjoy making someone wish they had never been born. I can just imagine him in a secret police force, somewhere where they pick on innocent people and throw them into stinking prisons. I've seen programmes on telly with people just like him.

The lesson begins and Mr Dorner pulls down the screen and switches on the OHP. The first transparency is of the monster Cerberus, the three-headed dog that guarded the underworld. The next... I don't know what the next is meant to be because in bold print there's this silly rhyme:

'They seek him here, they seek him there, the Binbags seek him everywhere. Is he in heaven, is he in hell, that damned elusive Pimpernel.'

'Binbags,' snorts ice-cool Sally in the back row, 'I haven't heard them called that before.' None of the Bins turn round or say anything to her, too scared. Pity she's not on our side but she doesn't care about anything really. She's leaving soon; thinks this school is a waste of time.

Mr Dorner isn't in a hurry to turn off the projection. He stares at it, his head on one side.

'I don't think we need that one, Mr Dorner, do we?' calls out Jaco. 'Unless you put it there for a reason of course, Sir.' Sarcasm dripping from him like grease.

I wonder whether just for a moment Jaco thinks a member of staff might be involved.

'It reminds me of something,' says Mr Dorner, to no one in particular. 'Oh well, very strange. Don't know how that got there at all. And that funny banner. Same person I suppose.'

'Can we get on with the dog, Mr Dorner? Mr Pent don't like us to tell him our lessons have just been the teacher waffling on, if you know what I mean.'

Dorner looks as if, just for a moment, he would like to bite Jaco's head off but then he checks himself. Maybe life's too short, or jobs are too hard to come by for the likes of him, because he does get on with it. I look at my watch, two hours, and then it's action time. No sign of Blake, just as he warned. I hope he's had success with Cyclops.

A howl of laughter comes from the next class and I wonder if the Pimpernel has left some little rhyme for them too.

A moment later I see Sir Pent striding past the door and I swear his hair has turned pink. It would be funny except his face looks like murder.

'Pent's gone pink!' says Sally. 'I hear all the Binbags are going to have to dye their hair pink too. What do you think of that, Jackson?' She calls Jaco Jackson. No one else dares.

'Mind your mouth,' he snarls, but he doesn't look at her and she shrugs and returns to her work. Stef looks uneasy, so does Maggot. Something is happening and they don't quite know what it is.

I know what it is and so does the Geek.

The Pimpernel.

Chapter 26

Break.

Rumours all over the place. Bits of chaos in most classrooms: an exploding inkpot in 4B. I saw Miss Chirtle, their form teacher, hurrying down the passage with black splodged across her blouse. Dry ice smoking in through an air extractor that seemed to be working in reverse – that was in the lab. Everyone thought there was going to be an explosion and there would be no more physics for the rest of term: that was the cheering we heard earlier. The best one though was the Pimpernel's broadcast. How he had done it I don't know but he'd somehow rigged up tiny speakers along the passage, in the main entrance and in the hall and when Sir Pent turned on the light switch the broadcast started and it just wouldn't turn off. It was on a loop and it sounded just like Sir Pent in his whispery, oozy voice saying: 'This is Sir Stephen Pent speaking, school, and I'm a liar and a cheat, and I want my mummy.'

We all heard it and of course everyone was whispering to each other: *'What do you want?'* and replying *'I want my mummy.'* It was driving Sir Pent into a black fury. He had staff and the Bins on ladders up and down everywhere trying to find the micro speakers. It took them over half an hour to track the last one. They were all handed in to Sir Pent who stamped on them, one after the other, then he grabbed a junior by the ear and yelled at him to sweep up the mess.

Only an hour and a half till the minister is due to arrive. Things are steaming but I'm still nervous and I'm hoping like anything that Blake has been successful with Cyclops.

I keep away from the Geek but I keep my eye out for Blake. Eventually he appears just before the bell rings for going back in to lessons. He looks the full nerd: fat tie, knot twisted a bit sideways so the collar of his shirt is buckling up, hair smoothed down so his ears seem to stick out more and the black-framed glasses of course. I see him explaining his being late to Mr Robestone, but Robestone's not listening, his eyes are scanning around looking for trouble, probably trying to figure out which of us is the Pimpernel!

I hear Robestone saying: 'Don't waste my time, Blake. Go on! Go away!' and Blake turns away, sees me, and makes a discreet signal for me to follow him, and then when he hurries off towards the changing rooms, I follow.

We have about ten seconds before a junior class comes in to change for P.E. 'Did you get to Cyclops?' I ask him.

'Yes. Fingers crossed he's pie-eyed by lunch. You and Minou all set?'

'Yes. Eighty minutes.'

'Good luck.'

And then the juniors come streaming in and Blake is somehow over by the washroom, combing his hair. I go out and he follows me half a minute later.

I just can't concentrate through the next lesson and I'm ticked off about three times. Jaco, Stef and the Maggot are all absent, probably with all the other Bins rehearsing something that'll give the impression we're this fantastic beacon school and not a hell-hole.

The lunch bell goes early and we are called class by class to go into the hall. We're last and end up standing at the back, which suits us since the Geek and I somehow have to slip out when the speeches start. When I look around I see that Blake is already gone; I don't think he can even have come into the hall. I wish we'd been as smart because at the moment Robestone is standing by the door that I had hoped to use for our exit. We'll never get past him.

Then I see the Geek edging her way forward, very casually. Like me, she's small and can mingle with the younger classes without getting noticed. Where's she heading? Of course, the kitchen exit. It'll be hard to slide by the cook and the two or three helpers he usually has with him but a whole lot easier than skinnying past Death-skull Robestone. I move over to the right and start to slip forward.

'Quiet!'

The school falls silent. I'm over right at the end of a row beside the wall; the Geek is two rows in front of me. She's got her wiry hair scraped into two pig-tails.

Sir Pent comes in. Somehow he's managed to get the pink out of his hair but he's nervous, you can see it. None of the draping himself around the microphone and whispering. He stands still and looks carefully around him, as if expecting a rocket to come firing out of the crowd, or a balloon to explode and fill the air with yellow powder. He has no expression on his face at all – a serpent doesn't.

The whole school waits.

'Very well,' he says. 'I sincerely hope there will be no more of these tricks. The perpetrators, I promise you, will be caught and there will be very, very serious consequences. Because of damage to school property...'

Damage? What damage?

'...the police have been called in. There may be formal charges, a court case, fines, prison...' He licks his lips and looks so snake-like I half imagine that the tip of his tongue is black and forked. 'Now in five minutes Jonathan Portiller...'

'Portaloo', mutters a joker in the middle school.

There's laughter and Robestone screams at the top of his voice – I've never heard anything like it, makes my teeth jar – 'That boy! Here! This instant!'

No one moves of course apart from those right beside the boy, who edge away from him. That's enough to give him away and two Bins go barging in and haul him out past Robestone, who follows them out of the main door. I don't hear anything because he shuts the door after him, but I can imagine a thump and a squeal.

'...the Minister of Education,' continues the Serpent, as if nothing has interrupted him. 'I expect you will want to applaud when he comes in and when he has finished speaking I expect you will want to stand quietly until you are given the signal to file out of school to the front gate where you will,' there's a little lift in his voice when he says 'will', 'where you will, in front of the press, want to wave him goodbye and perhaps give a cheer. Am I right?'

'Yes, Sir,' the school murmurs.

'Good,' he says, bringing his hands together in a soft clap; his face all the while remaining quite expressionless. The door behind the dais that he and the staff use to come into the hall opens and three figures appear. One of them I suppose is Mr Portiller. The Serpent glances over his shoulder and his face switches into a waxy smile. 'School,' he says into the microphone, 'Please welcome the Minister for Education, Mr Portiller.' There is a polite applause which suddenly gets louder as the Bins jab students to clap more enthusiastically.

Mr Portiller shakes hands with Sir Pent and steps up to the microphone. The applause dies down and then, as he takes a breath to speak, there is a sudden noisy whine of a motor and in through the window flies one of those little remote control planes. Brilliant guiding from whoever is at the controls, well, not whoever, it can only be Blake because trailing from the plane's tail is a banner just like advertisers sometimes use, except this one isn't promoting tyres or a supermarket chain. Instead it says, in bright pink on a scarlet background:

PRISON FOR PENT

There is uproar. The plane is dipping and whining around the hall, the minister is trying to speak into the microphone but all I can hear is: 'Excuse me. Excuse me...' The noise is tremendous as everybody is jumping around trying to catch the plane or the banner and bring it down; but the plane seems to know exactly what to do to avoid being caught. It comes within inches of destruction and then veers away at the last moment.

Blake must be able to see into the hall somehow. And then through the window up on the flat roof of the bike shed I spot a stocky figure in blue overalls. A workman fixing something? Not a chance; it's Blake, kneeling down and looking this way through mini binoculars. And there's a box on the ground in front of him – the controls!

I see the Geek in front of me turning round. I catch her eye. Time to go. The kitchen door is open: the cook and his helpers have come into the hall to see what's going on and have been caught up in the mayhem.

As we shove our way to the kitchen door, Sir Pent screams: 'There!' and when I look back I can see him flailing his way to the window. But Blake still has a card to play: the plane turns and with an ear-piercing whine dives down from the ceiling towards Pent and then crashes into his stomach. I don't expect it hurt but his face is a mask of absolute fury and he staggers back a pace or two, swatting at the toy like it's a wasp.

I don't see anything else because as everyone presses forward, me and the Geek slip through the kitchen door, race down past the stoves, out through the yard, into the changing room, grab my bag and then down the passage to the main entrance. Then, still flat out, not saying anything to each other, down the flight of stairs, down to the Swotshops. And Cyclops.

Chapter 27

The first flight is easy; we can see what we're doing and we fly down it, two steps at a time. We run past Swotshop One without even giving it a glance but at the top of the second flight, the Geek grabs my arm. 'Is there another way down?' she says.

'Might be. Don't think so, though.'

She doesn't let go. 'Do you think Blake will manage to join us...in time?'

She's worried. So am I but we can't stop now. 'He'll make it.'

'Did you see him up on the roof?'

'Yes. Come on.'

'Pent saw him too.' She's sort of hanging onto my arm. Not like her at all. 'He'll be after him.'

'Listen, Blake will have it planned. He said so. What's the problem, Minou?'

'I don't like the dark,' she says bluntly.

'Is that all!'

'I'm frightened of small spaces. Claustrophobia. The vent we have to crawl along. I'm just warning you. I might panic.'

'I'll go first if you like.'

'No, it's OK, I just wanted to say it. You know...in case. Anyway you have to do the rolling pin thing.' She takes a breath. 'Let's go.'

Level two.

Slower. Running the tip of my hand against the wall. Here. The stairway to the third level; except it's blocked! Bars. An iron gate. There was never one here before. There is now.

'What is it?' the Geek hisses at me.

I swing the little bag from my shoulder and pull out my Maglite. Just as I thought, a fat padlock and chain. 'They must be suspicious. Maybe one of the kidnapped winners said something.'

'No,' says the Geek. 'More likely a precaution because of this visit. Sir Pent wouldn't take any chances that the minister might want to take a wander round the school and then start asking awkward questions. He's just made it out of bounds. The point is, Patroclus, can you deal with it?'

Not the padlock, I can't; though I'm not bad with locks, used to take them apart but they take time to pick. I let the beam travel down the left side. The hinges. No problem. I give the Geek the torch while I get out the power driver and get to work. It only takes a couple of minutes and then we shuffle the gate round so it's balanced against the wall. We pause for a couple of seconds. No shouts of 'Oi!' or 'Who's that?' though we can faintly hear calling and yelling and running feet and somewhere a school bell buzzing – still chaos up in the main building. That's good.

Down we go. The last whispering sounds of the school disappear and we're in the underworld of creaking pipes and trickling and ghostly fingertip tapping. The Geek is so close to me I can feel her breath on my neck and the toes of her trainers keep tipping my heels.

I go carefully, counting the paces and then flick on the torch again. Spot on. 'The vent. You get on my shoulders and use this to get out the screws. It's not hard.'

I adjust the driver and show her the trigger. Then I pull out the two black Zorro masks Blake had given us. The Geek pulls a face and then takes off her glasses and gives them to me to put in the bag.

'Will you be able to see well enough?'

'I'll manage.'

We put the masks on. Amazing how it changes her, me too maybe: she's suddenly dark and a bit scary. She grins. 'We look the business, Patroclus.' And then she scrabbles up on to my back.

'Can you reach?'

'Just.'

She's quick. No messing. She hands down the grille and the driver and then she just lifts herself up, no bother. Stage one complete. I sling the driver in my bag and look up at the hole.

'You can't reach, can you?'

This I hadn't thought about, nor had Blake. Aaeee! That's my dad's wail in moments of despair when the lamb is overcooked or the chips burst into flames. I shake my head. How could I have been so stupid? If only Blake were here. But he's not. He's probably running around rooftops with half the school after him. It's up to us now, the Geek and me and she's up there and I'm down here - the dummy in the dark.

Then the Geek hisses at me. 'Take it!'

'What?'

'My hand, Patroclus. Wake up!'

I can see it now, her waving hand. I suppose I'm

not that heavy. The worst that can happen is that I pull her out of the opening and down on top of me. 'OK. Take the tool first.' I pull out the driver and hand it to her. Then I take a breath, crouch down and spring, swinging both my arms up, grabbing for her hand with both mine. I miss with the left but catch her wrist with my right and she catches mine. I'm surprised at how strong her grip is.

For a moment I'm hanging there, my legs flailing, and thinking this is getting to be a bit of a habit, with my other arm windmilling around trying to reach the lip of the opening. Slowly she inches me up a little, I get my left hand up on to the edge and then I'm half in, barging into her as she backs away. Stage two. Of course she's facing the wrong way now and has no room to turn. Brilliant!

'You're going to have to go backwards,' I whisper.

'I'm not stupid!'

'Sorry.'

So, practically nose to nose, we wriggle down the vent until we come to the turning. It takes forever, more than five minutes to travel what's not more than fifteen feet. At the opening the Geek undertakes a complicated manoeuvre to turn round and then she shuffles up to the grille, removes it and passes it back to me.

I can hear surprised voices from the room below and then, a bit like a seal slipping off a rock, the Geek dips down and slithers head first down into the light.

There's a loud 'Oof!' and then a crash as the door bangs open and I hear Cyclops. It's a repeat of last night's performance. Maybe he says the same thing every day. 'I warned you, didn'I? You brainy scumbags,' his voice is so slurred it sounds as if it's had olive oil drizzled over it. I peer down and there's the Geek, getting to her feet a little unsteadily.

'Worra hell are you?'

This is it. Stage three. The Geek takes a step back. She's thinking more clearly than me, leaving a space under the opening for Cyclops to stand, a target for me. I scrabble for the bag to get out my club and realise that I'm dripping with sweat again. Please don't let me drop it, I pray as I shift position to get my right arm over the opening, clutching the padded rolling pin by its wooden handle and feeling it slip a little in my palm.

Cyclops burps. 'I shaid who's she?'

No one answers.

'Orright, I'll see ter you. Throttle it out of yer.'

Cyclops comes lurching into view, shiny head stuck on bulging shoulders. A bulky body straining through his string vest. The reek off him is enough to make a pig gag. He lunges forward, faster than I expected and there's a squeak out of the Geek. 'Patroc— Uggh!' The back of his head is an unmissable target and I let him have it as hard as I can. The rolling pin lands with a crack.

Cyclops gives a startled: 'Uhf!' and half falls, half staggers forwards. My mother's rolling pin slips out of my hand and lands with a thunk on the floor. That was not in the plan and nor was this: the Geek gives a strangled yelp and realising that he hasn't let her go and having nothing with which to hit him again, I have no choice. The scream that's been bottled up inside me erupts like a war cry, 'Aaeee!' and I launch myself out of the vent and down onto his hairy shoulders.

He staggers, lets go of the Geek, whacks his right arm back trying to bang me off his back and begins to turn round and round with me hanging on, one arm round his thick neck, the other trying to get a grip on his bald head. Half a second later, a masked figure dressed in white overalls bursts in through the open door and hurls itself at Cyclops' legs. And, like a tree, he creaks and, slowly at first, he tips and then comes thundering to the floor.

I roll clear and help the Geek to her feet. The

masked figure is Blake of course, though the face he has on is a rubbery Charlie Chaplin. He staggers up, and I can see a bright trickle of blood dripping from his chin down onto the bib front of his overalls. 'How the mighty are fallen!' he says. I bet he's grinning under that silly face.

He dabs his sleeve against his chin, looks at the red stain. 'Seem to have got a biff. You two all right?'

'Yes. Think so.'

We're all a bit groggy but when Cyclops grunts and stirs, we snap into action again. I see beds. 'The sheets!'

We grab the sheets, rip them into strips and start winding them round the giant: hands first, then from his ankles up to his waist till he's like a half mummy. He starts to come to: 'I'll shkin you,' he snarls. 'I'll rip yer heads off.'

'Head next,' says Blake. 'Here we go, quick as we can.'

'I'll shtuff you down the nearest...' and the rest of the threat disappears into a muffled 'Pfhph' as the sheet gags him. We leave his giant nose free, but just to be safe we wind up the remaining part of him in the sheet strips. Only the incredible hulk could burst out of that lot. After a couple of attempts to kick out his bound legs and hump himself up into a sitting position, Cyclops slumps flat on his back and lies still.

Wearily we get to our feet and for the first time get a chance to take in our surroundings. The room is bigger than I imagined. Five bunk beds line three sides of the room. Where the fourth wall should be is an alcove opening into an adjoining room with lines of white-topped tables and banks of computers, screens flickering, printers whirring, paper spilling out into wire baskets already overflowing with print outs. Sitting at the computers but all looking our way are the missing competition winners. I count nine of them. Their eyes wide and round, their faces pale and frightened. Two of them are out of their seats, Charlie and the girl from yesterday, but they're not jumping up and down or grinning or hurrying over to us and wanting to shake our hands. At first I think it's just disbelief. We must look pretty strange.

'Who are you?' It's the girl, the one called Jenny.

'Friends of the Scarlet Pimpernel.'

'You what?'

'The little messages in school! The collapsing desk...' says Charlie. 'I know who you are,' pointing at me. 'You're...'

'No, you don't,' I say bluntly.

Blake is a little more diplomatic. 'Excuse the masks; but we'd rather not be known.'

'OK,' Charlie says slowly, looking at each of us in turn. 'I can keep a secret.'

'Good,' Blake says, dabbing a handkerchief awkwardly under his mask. Then in a more muffled voice, presumably because he's now got the handkerchief stuffed against his nose, 'Voila mes amis: Freedom! Liberty! Time to make a move. If you follow us, we'll get you home.'

But they don't move.

'What's wrong with you?'

'Sir Pent said he would do things to our families if we tried to run away – bad things,' says one boy. He doesn't look more than about nine years old. 'And we've got these things on our legs that hurt if we leave our desk without permission.'

'He said my dad would lose his job,' says another.

'He's really horrid. I think he'll kill us if we annoy him.'

Blake holds up his hands. 'Stop. Don't worry. Pent is going to prison. You're free; your families are safe.'

The Geek has been checking the young boy's ankle. 'Like an electronic tag. Probably gives stun shocks. Plastic. If we could find the terminal we could just switch it off, no problem.'

'Better than that,' says Blake, giving his nose another wipe, 'I have this.' He pulls a Stanley knife from his overalls. 'Who's first?'

In no time he's worked his way round all the prisoners. I'm half expecting a shock or sparks but Blake is careful and although there are wires buried in the plastic he manages to cut them one at a time so no one gets hurt.

'Now all we have to do is get up the stairs and out. There are TV crews and newspapers there. He can't do a thing to you once you're outside.'

The Geek reports that the stairs are clear. Blake lines them up and then tells them what they have to do. 'You follow the three of us. No one lingers behind. If anyone trips or falls, call out and we'll all stop. No one must get left behind. At the ground floor you go past us and run straight out to the gates. That's where the TV cameras are. Then you're safe. Stop for no one till you get there. We'll be right behind you. Everyone understand?'

They nod and say yes. The Geek and I exchange glances.

To the Geek and me, Blake quietly says, 'Just watch out at the top. With any luck there'll be so much chaos no one will notice this lot running for the gates; but we still might get trouble. Pent will try and stop them if he can and the Bins will be looking for us, me anyway. I'm a bit obvious in this now. I've a change of gear in a bag I stashed away outside. I can't get it till we're out so we need to be speedy.'

'OK.'

Rear guard, that's how he described us. I understand that. I'm just not sure how the three of us can face off all the Bins if they do come at us. Still I reckon Blake has a plan. He seems to have thought of everything so far.

We set off, all of us running; Blake, the Pimpernel, in his blood-splattered overalls in front, like some pied piper leading us all up from the underworld. The last leg. I think I'm on mine.

Chapter 28

Level two and we begin to hear sounds from above. There's the fire alarm ringing – perhaps Blake managed to set that off – and teachers shouting: 'Back into the classroom! Right now!' Feet pattering along the tiled floors.

The last flight: straight up to daylight and the entrance hall. Halfway, Blake holds up his hand and we stop. 'There are two Bins at the head of the stairs,' he whispers, 'their backs to us. We'll get them out of the way, then you charge through. Remember, as I told you before, straight through the front door, down the steps and to the main gate, and make as much noise as you can.' They nod their understanding. Most look pale, worried, but one or two are grinning. Charlie's one of them. Blake then arranges our rescued prisoners into pairs, biggest at the front. Then, with him leading and me and the Geek on his heels, we creep up the last few steps.

It's Stef on the left and Maggot on the right. Stef's got his hands in his pockets and is leaning against the corner of the entrance. Blake catches my eye and makes an arm round the neck movement and then to the Geek he points at Stef's ankles. Clear enough. We move in front.

Softly, softly. Two steps. I silently mouth: one, two, and on three, I grab Stef round the neck and the Geek tangles his ankles. Bursting up behind me comes Blake who shoves the startled Maggot sideways. As Stef falls down, the prisoners charge out, yelling their heads off, shoulder to shoulder, in a tight scrum, straight straight across the hall. Terrified of being crushed, the two Bins scuttle out of the way on their hands and knees and disappear into the classroom corridor.

'Yaahhaa!'

'Pim-per-nel!'

The prisoners hurtle past Robestone, shoving him to one side so he staggers, as if he's having a fit, his cheeks fiery red, his mouth still open but no sound coming out. Then they're out into the daylight but it's not over for us. Racing down the classroom corridor, there's a whole gang of Bins. Jaco's in the front.

'Get that funny face!' he screams. 'Get 'im.'

I'm still scrambling to my feet, but Blake is up, facing the Bins and looking as calm as if he's about to take a photograph. The Geek steps up beside him. 'Off you go,' he says briskly. 'I'll catch up with you outside.' Neither of us move and I don't know whether he's actually aware of us or not, his head's down and he's fiddling with a little black gadget thing. Whatever he's going to do I hope it's effective and quick. There's a tidal wave of Bins three seconds away.

'Scag 'em!'

'Rip and bin 'em!'

'It's that Pimpernel fruitcake. I want his guts.'

I catch a half glimpse of Robestone sliding away, his back to the wall, fumbling with a mobile. 'Headmaster,' he's saying, 'Headmaster...' Where is Pent? And the minister? Through the open doorway I see a crowd by the front gate, vans, a TV crew and over the yelling, the sound of a police siren.

The Geek grabs my arm, and there he is, Sir Pent, looking down at us from the stairs. For a moment everything freezes and I get a snapshot of the whole scene and it's just like when I forced myself up on to the top board at the local pool: everything down below was so small and sharp, and I felt an ugly pain in the pit of my stomach. There's Blake, a Charlie Chaplin in bloodstained white overalls, facing the horde of pounding Bins; me and the Geek just behind him, black masks across our eyes, a couple of pint-sized Zorros and Pent, his face unmasked, all twisted up with fury, pointing a shaking hand at us.

'You've ruined me!' he's screaming. 'All three of you!' His hair is flopped down over one eye and there is a big rent down his jacket.

'I certainly hope we have,' says Blake, cool as you like. And as the Bins explode into the entrance hall, he makes one last adjustment to the gadget and then takes a step back so he's between the two of us. 'Oh,' he says, 'you stayed. Nice one.'

And at that moment something extraordinary happens: the Bins start to stagger, like they're running in sticky mud. Their feet make sucking, snapping sounds against the floor. One of them falls and then another trips over him and then the whole lot of them come slapping down like a set of skittles, a thick tangling mesh of elbows and knees and sharp cries of pain. I see one Bin, his red bandana slipped down over his eyes and his face squashed flat into the backside of a hefty thug. What a wonderful sight. 'Beware a Blake bearing gifts,' I hear Blake murmur to himself. And yes, all the Bins are down! All but Jaco. Which is weird but the odds aren't in his favour any more. It's one against three.

Jaco's no war-sucking hero and he's not that big either, not when he's on his own. He hesitates but he's angry too and with Sir Pent screaming at him to kill us, he makes a sudden dash for Blake, trying to grab him by his overalls and swing him off balance.

Blake is fast though. You would never think it normally, he makes out he's so clumsy when he's in his duff disguise but now he's nimble, like a dancer, or one of those boxers who swing their legs head high and kick. And that's what he does. He spins once, twice and then: whack! the side of his foot catches the startled Jaco square on his back sending him flying straight towards us. The Geek sticks out her foot and down he goes. No contest.

'Bin him!' shouts Blake, diving on Jaco and grabbing him in a bear hug.

Yes!

The Geek and I grab a leg each, and then the three of us wrestle him up into the air. I get a snapshot of his face. He just can't believe what's happening to him. And then head-down he goes into the bin by the door. What a moment: Jaco binned!

The other Bins are still in a mess, shoving and punching; struggling to get to their feet even though their runners are firmly stuck to the floor. One or two of the smarter ones have managed to take their runners off but they're not interested in us, not after seeing Jaco upended, his legs wagging like a white flag over the bin.

'I'll have you,' hisses Sir Pent backing up the stairs. He looks like he's having a heart attack, clawing the air in front of him as if somehow that would drag us into his clutches. 'I'll do such things...' Then I see he's got his eye on what's happening outside. Heart attack switches to panic. Then, in a sudden flurry he's gone, up the stairs and out of sight.

Pupils are beginning to come out into the corridor and seeing the tangled-up heap of Bins, are pointing and laughing.

'Let's get rid of him for good,' says Blake, pointing at Jaco's wagging legs sticking up out of the bin we dumped him in. So the three of us heave the bin up as high as we can, ignoring Jaco's muffled cursing, shoulder high until his feet are tipping against the door frame.

'One,' says Blake. 'Two! Three!' And we toss the bin and Jaco onto the top step, from where he goes spinning and rolling down towards the waiting cameras.

'Game over,' says Blake. 'Time for our exit.' We nip along the side of the building, peeling our masks off as soon as we're out of view. Not that I think they're likely to spot us with all the pupils now pouring out of the school, some climbing out of the windows, others coming out through the entrance hall behind us. Down at the gate there's a crowd milling around, lights popping and parents weeping as they fuss around the rescued competition winners. There are blue uniforms running towards the school now; looking for Sir Pent, and good luck to them.

'What was that with the Bins? Like magic,' I say to Blake.

'Sticky runners.'

The Geek looks at him. 'What do you mean?'

'Gave them all special Blake runners, don't you remember, all but Jaco, because he had a proto-type? The others came from a model me and Dad worked on. Soles that respond to a signal, start to melt into a sticky resin. Neat, don't you think?'

'I'd say.'

He grins.

We take one look back round the corner. The crowd at the gate has grown even bigger. Even teachers are running from the building now. And the Bins, barefoot, and arms up shielding their heads, stumble away from the jeering swots.

It's easy enough to make our way round to the back of the kitchens where Blake has hidden a small bag with his school gear in. He strips off the overalls, pulls on his shirt, trousers, tugs the already fat-knotted tie over his head, and then on go the goofy glasses and there he is, comb slicking back his hair, a wadge of little putty-stuff wedged behind his ears to make them stick out: no longer the Pimpernel but the King of All Nerds. And Minou and me: I guess she's the Queen of Geeks and me, nothing really, Mr Nobody, a mouse, Mr Invisible.

We shake hands.

'That was something,' I say.

He grins. 'Until next time.' Then he's off, in that dopey jogging run he uses.

'See you later, Patroclus,' says the Geek.

'See you.'

That's it then, I think, the Geek, the Greek and the Pimpernel, and we're all going our own way. My mother and father, what will they say when I come home so early? 'Michael, what is this story. On the radio, I hear it about your school...' And of course I won't be able to tell them, will I? So I'll say it was nothing, nothing like the great stories, no heroes...

The Geek goes into the school via the changing rooms. I hang around for a minute, then head off in the opposite direction, taking the long route round the school and this is where I see Sir Pent for the last time. He's got a half-open briefcase bulging with papers clutched to his chest and two very large policemen on either side of him. It looks almost like they're holding him up and for half a second I'm not sure whether they are arresting him or taking him off to hospital. But they have to be arresting him, don't they? You can't be that twisted and crooked and get away with it.

They don't see me of course. Head down, collar up. Hugging the wall. Keeping to the shadow. Michael Patroclus. Mr Invisible. Wouldn't say boo to a goose.

*

And that's how it was, how I remember it, how I wrote it down. Quite something. Staleways got a new headmaster and the Bins got demoted, mostly. Funny how some of them got re-appointed as prefects; maybe that's the way the real world works.

They behaved OK though. I reckon the Pimpernel gave them a bit of a fright. Good lesson that, that even if you're top dog you can still get bitten.

The next term, me and the Geek do our thing, walk to school together and nobody hassles us. She says she'll teach me to climb; I tell her I'm going to teach her to cook. I call her Minou now but I think of her as the Geek, not a word I use as an insult for anyone. Then at the end of term Blake left. His parents decided to move him. The factory is still there, of course, pumping out Blake runners. Blake said he would keep in touch, but that's the sort of thing you do say when you move on, don't you.

As for Sir Pent, he just seemed to disappear. My father said, 'That man, may his soul rot, is in prison, of course he is, Michael! What do you think! He is a bad man!'

But I never read anything about a court case. One time I even heard his slithering voice on the radio, at least I think I did. I told the Geek. She said, 'Some bad things don't go away completely, do they,

Patroclus?' Maybe they don't, but then it seems to me that the good things don't go away either.

And you know what, the day after this conversation, she and I received identical postcards. No message on either of them, just the little squiggled flower.

The Pimpernel.

THE END

Other Orchard Books you might enjoy

The Fire Within	Chris d'Lacey	978 1 84121 533 4	£5.99
Icefire	Chris d'Lacey	978 1 84362 134 8	£5.99
Fire Star	Chris d'Lacey	978 1 84362 522 3	£5.99
The Snog Log	Michael Coleman	978 1 84121 161 9	£4.99
Tag	Michael Coleman	978 1 84362 182 9	£4.99
The Poltergoose	Michael Lawrence	978 1 86039 836 0	£4.99
The Killer Underpants	Michael Lawrence	978 1 84121 713 0	£5.99
The Toilet of Doom	Michael Lawrence	978 1 84121 752 9	£5.99
43 Bin Street	Livi Michael	978 1 84362 725 8	£4.99
Do Not Read This Book	Pat Moon	978 1 84121 435 1	£4.99
Do Not Read Any Further	Pat Moon	978 1 84121 456 6	£4.99
Do Not Read Or Else	Pat Moon	978 1 84616 082 0	£4.99
The Secret Life of Jamie B, Superspy	Ceri Worman	978 1 84362 389 2	£4.99
The Secret Life of Jamie B, Rapstar	Ceri Worman	978 1 84362 390 8	£4.99
The Secret Life of Jamie B, hero.com	Ceri Worman	978 1 84362 946 7	£4.99

Orchard Books are available from all good bookshops, or can be ordered direct
from the publisher: Orchard Books, PO BOX 29, Douglas IM99 1BQ
Credit card orders please telephone 01624 836000
or fax 01624 837033 or visit our website: www.orchardbooks.co.uk
or e-mail: bookshop@enterprise.net for details.

To order please quote title, author and ISBN
and your full name and address.
Cheques and postal orders should be made payable to 'Bookpost plc.'
Postage and packing is FREE within the UK
(overseas customers should add £1.00 per book).

Prices and availability are subject to change.